S0-ABY-127

"You're Just a Frustrated, Bad-Tempered Shrew!"

Cam wasn't allowed to finish his tirade. Kate swung wildly and he stood with mocking insolence and took the blow squarely on the cheek. Then as she watched in shock, he reached out and jerked her against him with a punishing force. His mouth came down on hers and she seethed with impotent fury as his hands began to move over her body with an insulting thoroughness. He tightened his hold, bringing her into a shocking closeness, and when the kiss changed into something less aggressive and more seductive, she found her anger unaccountably draining away.

DIXIE BROWNING
grew up on Hatteras Island off the coast of North Carolina. She is an accomplished and well-known artist of watercolors, as well as a prolific writer.

Dear Reader:

At Silhouette we try to publish books with you, our reader, in mind, and we're always trying to think of something new. We're very pleased to announce the creation of Silhouette First Love, a new line of contemporary romances written by the very finest young adult writers especially for our twelve-to-sixteen-year-old readers. First Love has many of the same elements you've enjoyed in Silhouette Romances—love stories, happy endings and the same attention to detail and description—but features heroines and situations with which our younger readers can more easily identify.

First Love from Silhouette will be available in bookstores this October. We will introduce First Love with six books, and each month thereafter we'll bring you two new First Love romances.

We welcome any suggestions or comments, and I invite you to write to us at the address below.

Karen Solem
Editor-in-Chief
Silhouette Books
P.O. Box 769
New York, N.Y. 10019

DIXIE BROWNING
East of Today

Silhouette *Romance*
Published by Silhouette Books New York
America's Publisher of Contemporary Romance

Other Silhouette Romances by Dixie Browning

Unreasonable Summer
Tumbled Wall
Chance Tomorrow
Wren of Paradise

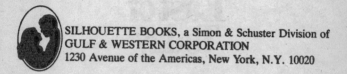

SILHOUETTE BOOKS, a Simon & Schuster Division of
GULF & WESTERN CORPORATION
1230 Avenue of the Americas, New York, N.Y. 10020

Copyright © 1981 by Dixie Browning

Distributed by Pocket Books

All rights reserved, including the right to reproduce
this book or portions thereof in any form whatsoever.
For information address Silhouette Books, 1230
Avenue of the Americas, New York, N.Y. 10020

ISBN: 0-671-57093-5

First Silhouette printing July, 1981

10 9 8 7 6 5 4 3 2 1

All of the characters in this book are fictitious. Any resemblance to actual persons, living or dead, is purely coincidental.

SILHOUETTE, SILHOUETTE ROMANCE and colophon are
trademarks of Simon & Schuster.

America's Publisher of Contemporary Romance

Printed in the U.S.A.

To Mary

East of Today

Chapter One

As a beginning to a new venture, the day hadn't been all that promising, Kate admitted to herself as she left the realtor's closet-sized office. An eight-hour drive would have been enough to put a damper on her usual ebullience without the flat tire, the spilled coffee on her brand-new yellow wraparound, and now this!

Sorry, the secretary had said, but Mr. Elliott was in Florida at a convention and wouldn't be back until the end of next week, but she could pick up the key from Mrs. Greyville at the main house.

What on earth was the main house? From the instructions, she was going to have trouble enough locating the bridge that led to the privately owned island where she had leased a house—what she had *thought* was the only one on the island. Mr. Elliott had been casual in his

9

descriptions, to say the least, but he had assured her he had the ideal location for what she had in mind, and since it was on a small island away from the village of Hatteras, she should have all the room and privacy she needed. The house was old, he had said, but the rooms were large, and he had arranged the removal of most of the furniture and the placement of four single beds in each of the two big bedrooms, plus one in each of the smaller rooms.

She found the bridge with none of the antici-pated trouble and paused at its rounded crest to view Coranoke Island for the first time. Perfect! Low and marshy on one end, wooded knolls over to the north, and a sandy shoreline upon which stood a tall, gaunt house that had not seen paint for generations, if ever. Its attitude of prim disregard for its precarious position at the edge of the water reminded her of an elderly spinster who lived in the apartment house she had just vacated and she promptly dubbed her summer home the Gray Lady. Fitting, too, as it belonged to a family called Greyville.

The sandy road split soon after leaving the bridge and she had no trouble determining which was the so-called main house. If the rows of tall oleanders, beginning and ending with Cape jasmines that were at least six feet around, weren't enough to set it apart, the sight of that large, shingled home with its well-kept gray trim and deep porches well furnished with brightly cushioned redwood furniture would have told her. Dignified without being at all ostentatious, the house crowned a wooded knoll as if it had been designed to shelter under the tall loblolly pines and the enormous live oaks and smaller bay trees.

So delighted with the appearance of the main house was she that she quite forgot to be disappointed at her lack of privacy on the island as she knocked on the paneled door.

After a minute she knocked again and looked around for a bell. As none was in sight and the weight of her long day was beginning to rest heavily upon her slight frame, she decided to see if she could rouse a response at the back of the house. She passed sweet scented nasturtiums and purple stocks mingled with ornamental onions and tomato plants and tried the next door she came to with similar results.

Darn! There was a car in the garage, an impressive gunmetal-gray sedan, so someone must be home. She wandered further and rounded a corner to hear a soft, teasing giggle. Following the sound, she saw a bikini-clad girl with red-gold hair and a terrific tan throw herself across a figure that was reclining in a huge hammock and begin to tickle and tease in a manner that brought a flush to Kate's face.

She was certainly no prude, but, all the same, she had obviously stumbled on a scene that was *not* meant for an audience and she didn't quite know what to do next. "Uh—excuse me," she began, noting with amusement the effect her interruption had on the couple. The girl was sprawled across the man's body, her fingers playing with the pelt of dark hair on his chest, and now she twisted around to stare open-mouthed at Kate while her partner in crime did his best to regain his feet.

A hammock is no place for sudden moves and Kate watched, amusement lifting the tiredness from her clear, gray-green eyes, to see who would get dumped first. She had taught art at a junior-senior high school long enough so that she ought not to be embarrassed at having come on the couple—what was it the kids called it these days?—making out? She couldn't manage to suppress a quick grin at the sight of that tall, somehow forbidding-looking man playing footsies with his wife.

Unfortunately, he saw her look and he was *not* amused. He disengaged himself from both blond and hammock with the agile ease of a trained athlete and stood before her, his tall, tanned body reflecting perfect physical condition, and not even his untidy dark blond hair could rob him of a certain air of authority. One dark, slashing eyebrow lifted in his rather aquiline face and Kate suddenly wished she had been more circumspect instead of poking around in strange back yards. She was uncomfortably aware of how she must look at the tag end of a rough day and so she turned to the man's wife, unwilling to suffer any longer the raking scrutiny of the man's hard amber eyes.

"Mrs. Greyville, the girl at the realtor's office said you'd have the key to the other house. I'd like to pick it up now, if I may? I'm Kate Brown—I've leased it for the season, you'll recall." Before the words had faded on the sweet scented air, Kate was wondering what sort of mistake she had made. Mrs. Greyville's expression was a combination of surprise and a sort of sly amusement and she cut her wide, china-blue eyes at her husband as if inviting him to share in the joke.

Whatever the joke was, the man was obviously in no mood to appreciate it. He glared at Kate, his hands resting insolently on hips left bare above low-slung homespun jeans, and his gaze left none of her untouched, from her last year's navy espadrilles to her coffee-stained yellow skirt, the skinny-knit navy top, and her dark brown hair, now escaping untidily, unfortunately, from its tortoise-shell clasp at the back of her head. He would have towered above her own five-feet-six even on level ground, but standing above her as he was, on the open redwood-decked porch, he had an unfair advantage, and Kate, who had driven four hundred miles in one day after a harrowing week of getting ready, suddenly ran out of patience. She had sunk almost the last penny of her savings into this venture, the lease being the largest part of it, but there had been advertising and brochures as well as other expenses and she was in no mood now to play games over a key with some petty tyrant.

"The key, if you please," she snapped, staring him right back in the eye with her most quelling look.

"Mrs. Greyville isn't here at the moment, but if you insist, I'll see if I can locate the key. I don't suppose you'd consider giving up the lease and finding other accommodation?"

"Of course I wouldn't! I was given to understand that this was about the only place suitable for my needs on either island and I paid a whacking good sum for it. I assure you, I have

an official, airtight lease with all the whereases
and hereinafters in place, and I'm not about to
give it up and start all over again!"

With the tightening of an already grim-looking
mouth, he turned and slammed into the house
while she waited there beside the porch, uninvited to come up and have a seat. Uncomfortably aware of the scrutiny of a pair of rather
vacant-looking blue eyes, she deliberately studied the distant shoreline until she was drawn to
return the stare. The girl was certainly rude, but
except for a petulant expression she was remarkably pretty.

No telling who she was, Kate mused as her
anger slowly drained away, leaving her feeling
tired and irritable. Mrs. Greyville was away and
the cat was at play; he probably had a whole
harem in reserve. From the looks of the man, he
could handle one with ease, she thought wither-
ingly. She had never trusted such blatantly
masculine creatures and she didn't now, but it
was none of her business what he did as long as
he stayed on his own side of the island.

The idea brought another unexpected flush to
her lightly tanned face and Kate studied a
butterfly-inhabited lantana until she heard the
return of her reluctant landlord. Goodness, she
might have done better to have tried her hand at
a spot of breaking and entering. While reprehen-
sible, not to mention highly illegal, it might have
been more comfortable than topping off the day
with *this* little episode! She accepted the grudgingly proffered key with an equally grudging
mumbled thanks and stalked away.

Climbing back into her car, Kate found herself
wondering what the absent Mrs. Greyville was

like. It would take quite a woman to stand up to a man like that. Unbidden, the ruggedly hand-some face with its unwelcoming eyes followed her all the way back to Gray Lady and she put it down to the fact that she was feeling every day of her almost twenty-seven years. The downhill side of youth was supposed to be a particularly susceptible time, she had read somewhere, and certainly nothing in her rather tame experience had prepared her for such blatant masculine virility. Lord help her if, unlikely as it was, such a force was ever aimed in *her* direction!

The Gray Lady, for all its unprepossessing appearance at the edge of the lapping waters of the Pamlico Sound, suited her purposes admira-bly. She had carefully selected from among her applicants so that she could distribute the sexes evenly into the two large bedrooms, more like dormitories now, and the living room would be perfect for an indoor studio. The one bathroom was ancient but adequate and the kitchen was something from a Victorian nightmare, but she had no doubts that Annie could cope. Annie had been delighted to come out of retirement for such a venture, and keeping up with the needs of nine artists would be a cinch for the woman who had run the school cafeteria almost single-handed for twenty years.

At the end of the lush row of oleanders that bordered the drive to the other house, Kate saw a discreet sign announcing the house as Bay Oaks. Hmmm. Slightly obvious, but better by far than most of the quaint-cute names she had noticed on the cottages on the way down to Hatteras. Well, unless her directional knob was sadly out of kilter, Gray Lady was west and Bay

Oaks was east, and never the twain should meet. She had come far enough east, anyway, after first considering the merits of establishing herself in the mountains of North Carolina and then settling for the drawing card of the Cape Hatteras National Seashore Park.

The water was deliciously hot, for she had lighted the pilot light on the heater first thing. She soaked thankfully in the claw-footed old tub, her feet propped up on the rim, and somewhere between allowing herself to acknowledge the fact that her delicate ankles and feet were among her best features and wondering if Annie would be able to cope with the laundry on the monstrous machine in the pantry, she wondered what Iola and Frances were doing now. She must remember to call her sister France, now that she had decided to go for a stage career in all seriousness. The name Frances Brown had been examined for star quality and found lacking.

Kate sighed and squeezed a sponge full of scented water over her shoulders. She missed them already. Iola had been divorced since Kate was fifteen and France nine and they had more or less raised each other since then. Kate, artistic temperament notwithstanding, had been by far the most practical of the trio, and she had worked at one thing after another to augment her mother's small annuity and to put herself through college. Iola added to their tight budget with the occasional sale of an article, for she was a free-lance writer of the freest sort. It was a source of constant amazement to Kate that editors seemed to like her style enough to over-look the fact that she had very little actual knowledge of her subject. The small checks were balm to an ego that had suffered, first from rejection by a womanizing husband and then from the slight limp incurred when she had rammed her car into the rear of a police car on her way to an antiviolence demonstration.

France was almost twenty-one now, and truly beautiful. She resembled their mother, their blond hair and brown eyes remarkably alike in spite of the thirty-years difference. Kate was the plain one, with her unremarkable features and average coloring. The fact that more than a few men had found her well worth pursuing did nothing to change her mind about her own appearance, nor did it bother her that she lacked her sister's beauty. She was fortunate enough to possess a marketable talent as well as a practical business head, and at the end of the summer session Kate fully intended to have saved up enough to send her sister to England, where she would audition for acceptance into the London Academy of Music and Dramatic Art.

She allowed the water to gurgle its way down the drain while her mind touched lightly on another factor in her decision to leave the school and strike out on her own. Hal Brookwood.

With a mutter of impatience, she scrubbed herself dry with a thick towel and stepped into her yellow lawn pajamas. They smelled faintly of a wild-flower sachet she favored and she inhaled appreciatively. She indulged in few luxuries—indeed, she had never been able to afford them—but Iola, disdainful as usual of the economies Kate tried to enforce, had presented her oldest daughter with sachets, lotion, and talc in the wild-flower fragrance, and Kate hadn't the heart to remonstrate with her. Lord knows what the two of them would get up to while she wasn't there to keep an eye on them. They were alike in their rather childlike approach to the realities of life as well as in their looks.

Almost too tired to sleep after making ten beds, Kate suddenly remembered that the last meal she had had was the hamburger and coffee early in the afternoon at Manteo. She had yet to shop for groceries but there were still two of the hard-boiled eggs she had brought from home and possibly a little of the coffee left in her thermos, if she could stomach it lukewarm.

She discovered a banana, the color of a prune but sweet and filling nevertheless, and she had just cracked the second egg, seated at the red Formica table in the kitchen, when the door opened to admit her landlord. At least, she had just assumed he was Mr. Greyville.

"You *are* Mr. Greyville, aren't you?" she asked, intent on getting to the bottom of the situation before chastising him for entering without bothering to knock.

He crossed the kitchen uninvited and pulled out a chair, swinging it around backward before dropping into it. "Right. Cameron Greyville, Miss . . . Brown, was it? I just now discovered the details of your lease from my grandmother, and since your light was still on, I thought we might discuss it."

Still indignant at his late intrusion, she was totally forgetful of her own casual attire, and she

glared at him balefully, prepared to do battle for
her legal rights.

"Look, I'll lay my cards on the table, Miss
Brown. The agent evidently misplaced my last
instructions, which were *not* to rent the house
this season, because I intend to spend a great
deal of time here and I need peace and quiet.
When I tried to reach him tonight I was told he'd
gone off to some convention or other."

At least he seemed in a more amenable mood,
Kate thought wryly, intent, no doubt, on talking
her around. He looked as if no one had ever
dared say no to him and she tried and failed to
conquer a grin of amusement when she remembered this superior creature, his well-cut chinos
probably costing more than she paid for a whole
outfit, as she had last seen him, with the cow-
eyed, pink-haired girl draped across him in the
hammock.

He hadn't missed her grin, nor was he used to
being a source of amusement—not that she
cared one whit. "Look, I can arrange for you to
have accommodation at a motel for the entire
summer for the same amount you would have
paid for this old place," he told her with a
disparaging look around at his own property.
"Shall I make the call?"

Under his rather prominent brow, those eyes
she remembered as golden brown looked almost
black and completely expressionless.

"Sorry. It wouldn't suit me at all. Besides, I've
had the agent replace the bedroom furniture
with cots and store the living room things to
make way for my tables. The place is perfect for
my needs and we're all set to start, so thanks,
but no thanks."

"We? I was under the impression that you were alone, Miss Brown. It *is* Miss?" His glance touched her hand and her fingers clenched involuntarily.

"Day after tomorrow, Mr. Greyville, there will be nine others besides myself staying here," she informed him with the aplomb due her position. She might not be *Mrs.* Kate Brown, but she was sure enough Kate Brown, A.W.S., and in *her* circles that stood for a darned sight more, signifying, as it did, her hard-earned inclusion into the nation's most prestigious watercolor society.

She was unprepared for his explosion. "Nine! Nine people living here? Good Lord, why?"

"Ten including myself, Mr. Greyville, and what do you mean, why? Because they're paying good money to spend two weeks down here, that's why," she explained testily.

"You mean you're subletting? Taking in roomers?" He stood and she wished he hadn't because the ceilings were tall, but, all the same, he made the room shrink alarmingly.

"No, I'm not taking in roomers," she told him with exaggerated patience. "At least, they'll be rooming here, but only because they'll be studying watercolor with me every day for two weeks, and then they'll leave and another group will take their place. Why else would I have needed a place this size?"

"Studying watercolor!"

You'd have thought she had contemplated opening a school for tone-deaf trumpeters. He obviously was no art lover, no matter what else he was.

Her small store of patience ran out. "Look, I explained to your Mr. Elliott when I . . ."

"He's not my Mr. Elliott!"

"Well, it's hardly *my* fault if you can't keep up with your own property! I leased this place in good faith for a legitimate business venture and all my papers are quite in order. I don't *think* you'll be able to find a loophole, Mr. Greyville—no matter how badly you want me out of here. And now, if you *don't* mind, I'd like to go to bed!" It was only then that she realized she had been sitting there in her thin cotton pajamas, her hair twisted into a damp-edged knot on top of her head, and the realization must have come to him at the same time, for she felt his glance drop down to touch her throat and the roundness below. Once more she felt the hot color rise to her face and she was furious with herself!

This was getting to be ridiculous! Already she had blushed more in one day than she had in the past fifteen years.

"Why couldn't you have stayed home and taught your painting classes?" he demanded, still unwilling to give up.

"For the simple reason that to attract people who are willing to pay top prices, you have to have more than one drawing card."

"The island being one," he sneered, "and I suppose *you're* the other?"

"You're darned right I am!"

"At least you're open about it. I've yet to meet a woman who didn't want to know, first, how much she could get and, second, how little she could give in return!"

Which seemed to Kate a harsh judgment for

trying to make a living. "Does that go for your
little hammock mate?" she asked sweetly, her
eyes glittering with righteous indignation.

"That, Miss Brown, is none of your business!"

"Well, all I have to say is that any poor fool of a
woman who's interested in you would *have* to be
after your money, because you obviously don't
have anything else to offer her!"

She flinched from the flaring of his nostrils
and the sparks that shot from his eyes, too late
aware that it could be exceedingly dangerous to
short-circuit the temper of a man like this.
Before she could begin to make an apology,
however, he had turned on his heel and left,
slamming the door behind him expressively.

Long after she crawled wearily between the
cool white sheets, she was aware of something
tingling in the atmosphere that hadn't been
there before. It was the feeling of expectancy
one senses sometimes before a severe electrical
storm.

She awakened early the next morning completely restored. The bedroom she had taken as
her own was close enough to the water so that
she could lie there and watch the reflections of
the sun dance across her painted white walls,
and suddenly, for no reason at all, she felt like
throwing wide her arms and embracing the day.
Somehow she seemed to have shed more than a
few of her concerns along the way yesterday,
and she didn't mind admitting to herself that it
was going to be marvelous not to have to deal
with Iola's impetuous and sometimes irrespon-
sible doings or wear herself out trying to keep up

with France's harebrained schemes. The last thing she had had to do before she left was to convince her younger sister that it was *not* a good idea to move into an apartment with a boyfriend just because he told her a male roommate was protection against unwanted followers.

France's beauty and her headstrong tendencies had been cause for more than a few headaches over the past few years, but Kate hoped she had convinced her that there was something to be said for the old-fashioned virtues. Of course, she had come in for her own share of ridicule, but she had taken it in good form. After all, one didn't reach the advanced age of twenty-six and a half without one or two offers, and Kate had been able to speak with some authority on the foibles of the male animal. The fact that she, herself, had never been sorely tempted she preferred to sidestep in her heart-to-heart discussions with the impetuous France. Maybe she was more fastidious than most, although she preferred to think of herself as just too romantic for the men she met in art school, who considered anything that lasted longer than a single date a meaningful relationship.

So she was well entrenched in spinsterhood! So what was wrong with that in this day and age? Four hundred miles away from her more pressing problems, she pulled on a pair of white jeans and a coral bouclé top and hurried outdoors to greet the day.

There were gulls wheeling and crying out everywhere and a fresh breeze off the water made her wrinkle her nose in delight at the

tantalizing blend of odors. Her shoes were filled
with sand before she had gone a dozen paces
and she stepped out of them and left them beside
the sandy path. She was determined to explore
something of her surroundings before heading
for the grocery store in Hatteras to stock up for
her coming hoards. This was her last free day for
the next two weeks.

There was no sign of life at Bay Oaks and she
allowed herself that small feeling of superiority
due one who was up with the sun as she skirted
the shoreline past dew-wet saltwater grass and
a thick cluster of fragrant wax myrtle. She came
to a small, weathered wharf and slowed down to
admire the reflections of the two boats moored
there—one a sleek new fiberglass runabout, the
other a wooden skiff that looked about the same
age as her own Gray Lady. She might be able to
borrow it sometime. It would be fun to explore
the coastline and see the island from the vantage point of that low-lying shoal she could see
from where she stood. Even as she watched,
another ludicrous-looking pelican flopped down
to join those already inhabiting the strip of sand.

"Hello there," called someone from behind
her.

Turning easily, she saw a tiny gray-haired
woman in orange pants and a wild-print smock.
She was carrying a trowel in one hand and a
basket in the other, and with a bright, eager
expression on her impish face, she hurried over
the remaining few yards of sand and extended
the hand that held the trowel. "I heard you'd
arrived. Hope you didn't have any trouble getting in. I was gone, you know. Garden Club

meeting. Look!" She held out her basket. "Bottlebrush. It's Australian, they tell me. Going to try it in the shelter of the house. What do you think?"

Bemused, Kate held out her own hand and touched the extended garden tool while the other woman continued talking about her exotic plans for reforesting the island. Who was she? The gardener? The housekeeper? She must be over seventy for all that she acted and dressed a quarter of that.

"So you're Kate Brown, hm? Not at all as I pictured you from your signature on the lease. Know anything about graphology? No, I thought not. Thought you'd be older, skinnier, spectacles, print dresses, and tennis shoes, you know? Glad to see you're not. Come up to the house for some coffee? I haven't had mine yet—wanted to get these seedlings out before the sun could blister them, but I'll stuff 'em in the refrigerator."

The other woman had turned and begun walking back in the direction of Bay Oaks, confident that Kate would join her. But Kate held back doubtfully. Whatever the connection this woman had, she didn't think the owner of the island would welcome an intrusion at this early hour, or any other, although after last night she owed him one.

"I don't think I'd better, Mrs. . . . Miss . . ."

"Oh, call me Dotty. Cam says I am—dotty, that is. My grandson, Cam Greyville. You must have met him when you picked up the key."

Realization dawned. "Oh. Then you're Mrs. Greyville!"

"Dotty Greyville. Coffee now? No? Oh, don't hold back on Cam's account. He won't bite while I'm around, and that so-called secretary of his won't be up until someone tosses a stick of dynamite into her room!"

"Yes, well, all the same, I think I'll stay out and enjoy the morning a few minutes more before I head for the grocery store," Kate said, not wanting to offend the first friendly face she had seen on the island.

Dotty dropped unceremoniously onto a lichen-covered bench under the oaks and Kate followed suit, amused to see on the gnarled, dirt-covered hands a collection of gems that would have paid her salary several times over. They fell into a discussion of Kate's plans and then Dotty went on to talk about her grandson. "Stays up there in New York as long as he has to, then he slips away down here where he does his real work. He's the chief design engineer, you know— Greyville Electronics. Not that he has to turn a hand, but he's got the sort of brain that loves to tackle a problem and come up with the solution—and the harder it is, the better he likes it. Why, even as a boy, he'd get his teeth into something and sit around the house with his eyes half closed for days, and you'd think he had given up. Then all of a sudden he'd swing into action, and presto!" She paused to take out a cigarette and fit it into a five-inch jade green holder and Kate was glad Iola couldn't see her. Iola went in for the dramatic effect and if she saw how effective that particular whimsy was, she'd start smoking, and Lord knows they couldn't afford it.

"He loves it down here—says it's the only place he's found where he can hear himself think—but that pink-haired popsie comes trailing on down after him every chance she gets, and Lord knows how anybody can concentrate with her and her radio around! Got no more brain than God gave a green apple but Cam says she can take down technical terms a mile a minute without missing a trick!"

"She's awfully pretty," Kate ventured.

"Hmph! Her type's easy enough to find. They flock around him like a swarm of mosquitos on a still night. He'll put up with it for a while, then he'll shoo away the whole swarm. Likes 'em good-looking, like all men, but he's not the marrying kind, thank the Lord!"

"You don't want him to marry?" Kate asked curiously, a little dismayed at her own interest.

"Not one of those, I wouldn't. How'd you like to be shut up in the house for a long rainy spell with a pink-haired, half-naked female who talks baby talk? You'd see Miss Bebe Gonlon hightailing it back up north if all of a sudden the bottom fell out of Greyville stock, and don't think Cam doesn't know it. He might have his head in the clouds when it comes to those electronic thingamabobs he dreams up, but his feet are planted firmly on the ground."

I'll just bet they are, Kate thought grimly. If she ever saw a man who looked as if he could hold his own against any odds it was Cameron Greyville, and he didn't strike her for one minute as a dreamer. She decided later on, when she was putting away enough food for the first few days after spending an alarming amount for groceries, that she was going to like Dotty Greyville very much. The old woman with her pixie haircut and her outspoken opinions was something of a tartar, but then Kate had never particularly cared for namby-pambies.

Chapter Two

The next morning Kate was up again before six, determined to spend a few hours of glorious solitude before the descent of the multitudes. She had remembered to mention the skiff to Dotty yesterday and had acquired permission to use it. Now she tossed down a glass of tomato juice and let herself out the back door, noticing, for the second day, a low cloudbank hovering over the Sound. It had dispersed yesterday under the heat of the sun and she only hoped it would today. The last thing she needed to launch her project was a few days of dismal rain!

The skiff handled well and was reasonably dry. No expert with the oars, Kate nevertheless managed to work her way to the shoal she had spotted earlier, and she rolled her pants legs up before jumping over the side to haul her boat up onto the hard sand. It refused to be shoved more

than a few inches, for it was far heavier than it
looked, but she gave it a testing shove and
decided it was secure.

There was not a whole lot to see, other than a
few broken shells and hundreds of bird tracks.
She walked slowly around the perimeter studying these and the patterns made by eddying
currents, picking up a bleached clam shell now
and then and skipping it across the water.
Overhead a single gull protested the invasion of
his privacy and she grinned up at him. "You,
too? You founding father types seem to think you
own the world around here. Fie on you!"

She walked on, her grin fading. So far, with
the exception of Dotty Greyville, she had found
scant welcome here on the Outer Banks. It took
time, of course, to become established in any
new neighborhood, but she had felt so certain of
Coranoke Island—almost as if something were
urging her on to make the move. She had been
drawn by a sense of expectation, as if something
wonderful awaited her, and she hated to have it
spoiled for her before she even had a chance to
discover what it was.

Cameron Greyville! The man would obviously
prefer her absence to her company, for all the
good it would do him. Aggravating man, with
his arrogant, overbearing manner—as if no one
else had any rights at all! Talk about your
egocentric types! Hard to imagine his being
Dotty's grandson, but then, everyone was somebody's grandchild and like didn't always breed
like.

She concentrated for a while on the colors,
mentally selecting a thin wash of alizarin crim-

son for the underpainting of the sky to get that faint, cool pinkish cast. Cerulean—no, perhaps the faintest tint of thalo blue. She painted in her mind, arguing with herself as she sat on the hard-packed sand, arms clasped around her updrawn knees as she gazed off across the Sound to the invisible mainland.

It was some time before she recognized her name among the ambient sounds—the gulls and terns, the lap-lap of water, and the impatient buzz of a distant outboard motor. She shaded her eyes and searched the horizon before she saw the two figures on the wharf of Coranoke. One was waving and the other one was Cameron Greyville. She'd have recognized that lean, powerful build anywhere—not to mention the impatient stance—and the man beside him looked terribly familiar as well.

Hoping against hope that she was mistaken, she turned toward the skiff, only to see it drifting provocatively just out of reach. Darn! She supposed she should have thought of tides, but she was far more familiar with lakes than she was with Sounds and it hadn't occurred to her that the water could rise to any appreciable level in such a short time. She began wading out, peering carefully through the turbid water to the sandy bottom. So far, so good—only the boat seemed to be moving slightly faster than she was, and she daren't go faster.

The air was suddenly rent by an angry roar and she looked up, startled, to see the runabout swerve away from the wharf and head for the shoal. Oh, great! Just what she needed to foster good neighbor relations. There was only one

man in the cockpit and she had no trouble
recognizing Cameron's frown even with the
aviator-style dark glasses.

"Jump in," he ordered over the muffled roar,
giving her barely time to settle herself into the
other seat before peeling off to circle the skiff.
He scooped up the bowline and made it fast to a
cleat behind him, and as he turned to the
controls again, he spared her a look that left her
in no doubt as to his opinion of people who
borrowed property and then failed to look after
it. The fact that he was absolutely right didn't
make it any easier to take either.

The ride was completed in utter silence, if one
discounted the angry roar of all that shiny
horsepower. By the time they reached the
wharf, Kate was even glad to see Hal's friendly
face, although he was one of the reasons she had
needed to get away from home.

"Katie, baby, what on earth were you doing
out there by yourself? I knew darned well you'd
do something foolish as soon as you got off here
on your own."

"Hello, Hal. It's good to see you, too." She
climbed out of the runabout, ignoring Hal's
outstretched hand. Cameron didn't offer to help
her. "What are you doing in these parts? I
thought you'd be all tied up at the store." She
suffered his kiss with perhaps a bit more
warmth than she would have had not Cameron
Greyville been standing there eyeing them with
that infuriating condescension.

She had met Hal Brookwood three years before and he had been her most persistent admir-
er. She dated him occasionally, because they
saw each other whenever she went into his

bookstore to buy art supplies and it was easier to give in to him than to go on thinking up excuses. Lately, though, she had sensed a more serious note in his attentions and she had been glad of a legitimate excuse to end the light relationship.

"I left things in good hands. Sal Turner is working out even better than I hoped and I thought it would build confidence if I left her to manage for a few days on her own. Anyway"— he looked at her with heavy significance—"I missed you even more than I expected to. What about you?" There was a spaniel look in his large, dark eyes and she hated herself for not caring more, but there it was. His pleasant, ordinary face didn't make her heart beat a bit faster and his kisses, as few as she could get by with, left her feeling nothing but a slight revulsion. There was something obviously missing in her makeup, and she sighed now as she wondered if she were being a silly, romantic fool for even dreaming of anything more.

They strolled back toward Gray Lady and she felt as if eyes were burning into her back, but when she paused to scoop up her shoes and happened to glance back toward the wharf, Cameron had already gone. Hal was distinctly put out when she told him that he'd have to find a room at a motel in Hatteras, but she explained that her classes and her housekeeper were all due in sometime today and there just wasn't any room left over. She supposed she could have managed to squeeze in one more, but it served him right, showing up unannounced this way. She'd have little time for entertaining, as it was, and he'd have to fend for himself.

The first couple came just after lunch and

then cars seemed to roll across the old wooden
bridge with a paradelike regularity. It hadn't
occurred to her that they'd be taking up so much
room and she had to spoil one of the nicest views
in order to find parking space for them all.

By dinnertime everyone had arrived except
Annie and Kate was beginning to sort them out.
Two women from Virginia were veterans of a
good many workshops, and then there was an
enthusiastic beginner and a perfectly gorgeous
would-be fashion designer who wanted to perfect her skills with the medium. Stella Wright,
the lovely titian-haired designer, immediately
turned full batteries onto the only male under
forty and Kate watched with amusement as they
sized each other up.

Tony Palani had roared across the bridge in a
red Aston Martin and halted a few inches from
the edge of the water, just as if salt didn't rust
metal. She had warned him about the tide but he
had waved a casual hand as if to say, Easy come,
easy go, and Kate had shrugged and returned to
the others. Tony, she had seen at a glance, was
the sort to get along wherever he was. A good-
looking brunet whose clever eyes had quickly
evaluated the whole group and returned to settle
speculatively on Stella Wright, he tossed his soft
leather bag and his canvas paint case onto a
table and made himself at home.

They were putting together a meal from cold
cuts and salads when Cam appeared in the
doorway to tell Kate she was wanted on the
phone. He stood there, his coiled-spring body
almost filling the opening, and looked the group
over derisively, his eyes finally returning to
where Stella was leaning back in a chair sipping

a tall drink while the others fixed the meal. She had pronounced herself the decorative rather than the utilitarian type and Kate had seen no point in arguing. She'd have to school herself to be more accommodating and to keep her rather warm temper under wraps.

She returned from her room with her shoes in her hand and slipped them on before following Cam across the clearing between the two houses. It was much more direct than going around by way of the oleander lined driveway in front. "She's not still hanging on, is she?" she called out suddenly with visions of a three-figure phone bill being forwarded from home.

He turned and waited for her to catch up. "No, there's an operator number for you to call. What makes you think it's a woman?"

"Oh, well, I just assumed it was Iola—my mother. She didn't say?"

"No, she didn't, but, as a matter of fact, it was a woman. I suppose with loverboy on the scene the odds were cut down. Unless you have a few more back home."

"You never quit, do you? For your information, Hal is not a loverboy," she snapped, trudging breathlessly along behind him as his longer legs ate up the distance.

"Don't forget, I had several minutes to get acquainted with him while you were day-dreaming out there on Pelican Shoal."

"I don't care if you had three weeks to get acquainted with him, Hal Brookwood is nothing to me but a good friend—not that it's any of your business—and besides, I was not daydreaming!"

He laughed and the sound fell unpleasantly on the peaceful evening air. Kate fumed. Unfortu-

nately, there was no way she could refute a
disbelieving laugh.

Dotty greeted her with an invitation to dinner.
She was wearing a purple and lime green caftan
that Iola would have loved and the hoops in her
ears were as big as bracelets.

"Thanks, Dotty, but I've got the whole crew
over there improvising something since our cook
is late getting here." She had time to catch a
quick impression of polished wood and gleaming
brass before Cameron handed her the phone and
she stood there studying a handsome arrangement of bayberry and cryptomeria while she
waited for the operator to connect her, and then
she was speaking to Annie.

"What happened?"

"Oh, Katie, you're never going to believe this,
but I'm flat on my back in Forsyth Memorial,
and I could kick myself up one side and down
the other! Here I've gone and let you down at the
last minute and I was looking forward to this
summer so much!" It seemed that Annie, in her
eagerness to get ready, had climbed the fold-
away ladder to her attic and attempted to bring
down a trunk single-handed. She was now un-
dergoing treatment for a slipped disc and would
be in the hospital for weeks and out of commis-
sion for no telling how long.

After assuring her that there was no problem
on this end, Kate went on to invite her to come
down and recuperate whenever she felt up to it,
but both she and Annie knew there was little
chance of that. She hung up the phone and
turned away dejectedly. How in the world were
they going to manage without her? Catering to
eight people—eight busy people—was a full-time

job, and Kate could only hope to find someone locally.

As she passed the open doorway of the living room, where Cam and his grandmother were having a pre-dinner sherry, Cam stood and offered her one. She shook her head and thanked him for calling her to the phone, and Dotty asked her if it had been bad news.

"'Fraid so. The woman who was to have cooked and kept house for us won't be able to make it, and my classes start tomorrow. I don't suppose you know of anyone I could hire to do meals and generally give the place a once-over, do you? I can handle the laundry myself if I have to."

"Maybe your good friend will stay and lend a hand," Cam suggested lazily, surveying her over the rim of his glass before putting it down on a handsome old pine drop-leafed table. "He looked the sort to turn a hand at most anything if the rewards were sweet enough."

"I'm afraid that won't be practical," she retorted bitingly, turning toward the front door at the same time that Dotty was summoned by a woman in an apron and cap.

"I'll see you out," Cam murmured, holding the screen open for her and following her out onto the wide, wisteria-shaded porch.

"That won't be necessary, thanks."

"It's as good a time as any to speak to you about your . . . artist friends." The pause was almost unnoticeable, but somehow insulting, for all that. "I came down to the island for peace and quiet and I'd appreciate it if you'd restrain the freer of the free spirits among them. The impromptu parking lot you've established will only churn up the sand, but let's not have any going and coming at all hours, especially the Latin lover type with the sports car. Dotty sleeps on this side of the house and I won't have her disturbed."

"Is that quite all?" she said tightly.

"No. While your crew looks harmless enough on the surface, keep in mind that this is a pretty conservative area and any wild parties or outdoor life classes—unadorned, that is—won't go unnoticed. You might find yourself asked to move on if you prove an undesirable addition to the community. A word to the wise."

By this time Kate had come to a slow simmer and now she turned to face him squarely. They were well enough away from the front door so that there was little danger of Dotty's overhearing, something Cameron had probably taken into consideration. He wouldn't like to disillusion his grandmother as to his true nature, no doubt! "And now you listen here to me, Mr. Cameron Greyville. I don't know just who gave you the right to make snap judgments about people, but you're absolutely wrong about my friends! From what I've seen of *your* taste in companions, you don't have any room to talk! Any community that would welcome the fun and games *you* probably engage in would consider my crew pillars of the society!"

"And now who's making judgments? Let me tell you something, Kate Brown—there's a world of difference between the business community and the artists' colonies I know anything about! Believe me, I've heard a few tales about your sort!"

"Oh, have you now?" she baited. "I'll bet you

just pour over the tabloids looking for juicy
morsels, you self-righteous prig! I'll have you
know that my students are all at the top of
their professions—some of them teachers and a
few of them even sanctified bona fide business-
men like yourself! Believe it or not, even in the
wicked world of commerce, they're not all philis-
tines like you!"

"We'll see, Miss Brown, we'll see. Meanwhile,
just keep them away from this side of the
island—do you understand?"

"Oh, but . . ." The protest broke from her
before she could stop it.

"Oh, but?" he sneered.

"Well, do you mean we can't even paint from
the knoll or the grove over there on the other
side? The best views of Hatteras are from there
and I had planned . . ."

"I'll just bet you had, Miss Brown. I can see
the avaricious gleam in those cool, deceptive
eyes of yours when you even look at my place,
but you leased the old house and that alone.
Everything else is out of bounds! And, while I
think of it, stay out of my boats, too."

"Gladly, Mr. Greyville! I don't even care to
breathe the air in your vicinity!"

"Camsey," crooned a petulant voice from
overhead, "you woke me up. Must you quarrel
under my window?"

They both looked up in time to see the pinkish
blond, her face sleep-flushed and her delectable
body clearly revealed in a bra and half-slip as
she opened the louvered windows to lean out.
Beside her in the other window, an air conditioner droned away, dripping moisture into the
flower bed beneath.

"If you'd keep your windows closed when you're using the air conditioner, Bebe, you wouldn't have been bothered. At any rate, it's time to come down to dinner. Miss Brown and I have finished our little discussion, haven't we, Miss Brown?"

His mocking glance returned to Kate and she was ready with one of her own. If *that* were not a case of the pot calling the kettle black, she'd like to see one. She smiled sweetly up at him and said, "I'm so sorry we disturbed the peace . . . of your little friend. I'm not usually so noisy, but you know how it is sometimes when you get involved with undesirable company." She strolled away, her head at an unlikely angle and an irrepressible grin on her face. She had quite got over the misfortune of losing Annie's services, at any rate. For the time being, that was.

The grin had faded by the time she reached Gray Lady. Cameron Greyville spelled trouble for her. She was not quite sure just how she was going to get around his edict, but surely no one in his right mind would expect her to keep eight adults shut up indoors for two weeks. She wasn't sure just where her legal boundaries were, but she was certainly not going to relinquish any of her rights without a darned good fight. Even the thought of it brought a militant brilliance to her eyes.

The first class was conducted just over the bridge on Hatteras. Kate was able to size up the widely varied abilities of her students and consider the best approach to teaching them. She had found early in her teaching career that art could not be packaged and distributed arbitrar-

ily. It involved far more than technical ability.
And she discovered that first morning that her
students ran the gamut as far as technical
proficiency was concerned, which meant that
she had her work cut out for her in keeping them
all involved without slighting either end of the
spectrum.

Among the middle range were two students
who promised to become problems. Stella was
fairly proficient and could probably have
achieved exhibiting status but for a bone-deep
inertia that spilled over into every aspect of her
life. Her two interests, in order of seeming
importance, were men and fashion, and that
presented the next problem—Tony Palani.

In her years at college and since, this was not
the first time Kate had run across men of Tony's
type. It was, however, the first time she had had
to deal with one at close range. Tony was extremely good-looking in a dark, flashy way, and
he made quite sure everyone around realized the
extent of his wealth—or, at least, his father's
wealth. He had immediately set his sights on the
only two women he considered interesting—
Stella and Kate—and he let it be known that he
had a great deal to offer his lucky final choice.

As far as painting was concerned, he was an
accomplished hobbyist but depended rather
more on his charm than on any real ability, and
Kate was afraid that long before his two weeks
were up that charm was going to wear terribly
thin.

Hal was still in residence, having taken advantage of Annie's absence to move into her
room, and when he volunteered to lend a hand
with the chores, Kate had little choice but to

take him up on it, although she regretted being under obligation to him. Actually, she really needed his help, she discovered after the first day's classes for if teaching alone didn't drain her energies, there was the perpetual running back and forth supplying missing equipment and fetching sunhats or glasses or whatever else had been left behind when they trouped out to location.

Of course, they wouldn't have to go all that far if Cameron Greyville weren't such a beast about the whole thing. The idea of the best parts of the island going to waste while her little troupe had to trudge a mile or so in the hot sun or pile into cars to go even further afield! Right here at hand were marshes, wharves, woods, and beaches lovelier than anything they could find in Hatteras without invading someone's private property.

It only served to underline her feelings about men in general. While all her friends had found someone they could contemplate settling down with—at least for the forseeable future—she found men totally unreasonable. Either they claimed to be wasting away from unrequited love and wanted her to give up her career and devote herself exclusively to making them happy or they expected her to hop into bed with them with no commitment on either side. There had already been a few hints of the latter inclination on Tony's part, and the classes had hardly begun!

Never far from the surface of her mind was her landlord. There were simply no grounds for a relationship of any sort between her and Cameron Greyville—no common ground at all— and she only hoped they could avoid any further confrontations, for they seemed to touch off a wild animosity in each other that got worse with each exposure.

Hal departed early Wednesday morning after promising to try and make the trip again over the Fourth of July. It was a slack season at the store and he could afford to take a few days' vacation to add to the holiday. Kate simply nodded in resignation. No matter what she said, he'd come anyway. He was convinced that she loved him but was too proud to inflict the burden of her family on him.

Lord, if there was anything she was *not*, it was a martyr! She hoped to send France to school, yes, and she did feel compelled to add to the strained family resources perhaps more than her share, but then, she was the oldest child and the only one with a regular job. Besides, she was selfish enough to hope that this summer's venture would prove profitable enough to enable her to quit her job at the school and spend her winters painting. After teaching five days a week for a small salary and then spending far too much outside time on school-related projects, she had no creative energy left over for her own painting.

Of Cameron she saw nothing at all. She assumed his girl friend was still there, for she heard the almost constant blare of a radio and she couldn't imagine either him or his grandmother being that devoted to loud rock music.

Dotty strolled over one morning to look over the shoulders of the painters and she volunteered a few comments that indicated she was familiar with the medium. She made a few ribald comments about Bebe Gonlon's taste in music when a breeze brought the tinny sound across the bridge to where the class was meeting. "She's hanging on a lot longer than usual and I'm wondering how long Cam's temper is going to hold up. He's a patient man, but when he blows, watch out!" Dotty warned.

Kate smiled tightly and abstained from mentioning what she thought of Cam's patience. That was a commodity he reserved for a favored few, evidently. "We're treated to a free daily concert, especially since the wind has been in this direction every day this week," she told the older woman. It was as close to a complaint as she dared come and she only hoped Dotty would repeat it where it would do the most good. Her own musical tastes leaned radically in the opposite direction.

On the first day of the second week, Stella was absent from the afternoon class. She had skipped a few of the evening sessions to go out with Tony, but today Tony was very much in evidence, his good-looking face a little sulky as he set up as close to Kate as he could. It was Selma Kinfiled, one of the older women, who mentioned having seen Stella strolling across to Bay Oaks. Kate bit back her curiosity and tried not to glance up at the main house every few minutes. Perhaps Stella had only wanted to use the phone. As far as Kate knew, she was unacquainted with Cameron, and somehow she didn't seem the sort to spend an afternoon visiting Dotty Greyville.

There was this much to be said for teaching adults: if they didn't want to learn, one didn't feel obligated to force them. By the time dinner was over and they were clearing the tables for the evening critique session, Stella had not returned, and Kate wondered if something could have happened to her. They were well under way with an avid discussion of the use of maskoid, Kate having trouble keeping her mind on the subject at hand, when they heard a car rumble across the bridge and pull up out in front of Gray Lady. She looked up from her demonstration in time to see Stella and Cam enter. Stella had evidently found time to come back during the afternoon and change her clothes after morning class, for she was wearing a pink midi-length sundress that made the most of her flawless complexion.

"We went out to dinner," she announced as Cam came over and stood peering over Kate's shoulder. "Hope you didn't wait for me."

"Not at all," Kate replied coolly, flipping over the paper she had been demonstrating the masking technique on. "Did you have a nice evening?" She sounded peeved and she could have kicked herself!

Cameron reached past her and turned her paper back over, examining it with interest. It was a light, sketchy rendition of the shoreline, with white gulls and reflected boats contrasting with a deep blue-gray sky, and he murmured, "Nice. Do you really see it this way?"

"It's only one facet of the scene. You, of course, would prefer a photograph."

"No, I don't think so. You've picked out a rhythm of wind and water that livens it up quite a bit, but I think perhaps the gulls are overemphasized."

She was flabbergasted! Not only was his eye quick and discerning, he'd known immediately what was wrong with it.

"I was demonstrating a technique, if you must know, not working on the definitive seascape," she told him, her head held at a proud angle. The others were all too involved with their own work to be paying any attention to the small interchange, but Stella was taking in every word and her creamy little smile irritated Kate for no good reason at all.

Nor was Tony missing out on much. His dark eyes were flashing from Cameron to Stella, to Kate, and back again with a measuring gleam in their depths.

"If you'll excuse me, Mr. Greyville, I'll get on with the class," Kate announced, turning her shoulder to him as she tried to find something that needed touching up on her sketch. It was finished, as she well knew, but she had to busy herself at something while he was standing there looking so smug, and she succeeded in ruining it, overworking it completely while he gazed impersonally over her shoulder. She could have kicked the man!

"Oh, well, can't win 'em all," he remarked laconically, moving off with a casual wave.

Stella thanked him sweetly for the dinner, leaning over so that her light red hair brushed against his white sleeve, and she promised to be on the wharf at eight thirty the next morning.

So much for art lessons, Kate thought sourly. For a girl like Stella Wright, there was no contest when it came to choosing between slaving over a hot drawing board and hanging around with an attractive, fascinating man.

And then she caught herself up sharply. Since when did she consider Cameron Greyville an attractive, fascinating man? And what's more, why was she reacting to his presence like some gauche sophomore? He was no different from any other man. She hoped he'd trip over his big clay feet and fall flat on his condescending face!

Stella spent the remainder of her time in Cameron's company and Kate could only wonder what he had done with his secretary. He had a decided preference for redheads, it seemed, but at least this one was not a rock music addict. The airwaves had been satisfyingly quiet, now that she thought of it, and if she had trouble sleeping nights, it was certainly not for want of trying. She lay there long after the others had turned in and listened to the water music that seemed to come from right underneath her, and neither that nor the song of a disoriented mockingbird could lull her thoughts into behaving.

Tony made the most of Stella's defection by concentrating his practiced charm on Kate. His previous attempts at flirtation had been diluted when he was torn between the two of them, but now she found she had to put him in his place several times a day.

It was next to the last night and the evening critique had given way to a flurry of matting and hanging. Kate had posted several notices in Hatteras in hopes of luring a few tourists as well as any interested villagers to their one-day exhibit. It was a wind-up of the session and she planned it more for the fun of seeing public reaction to their work than any real hope of sales.

Exhausted after a day of trying to impart to

the students enough to keep them going on their
own, Kate had left them to it and wandered out
to the bridge to hang over the rail and watch the
stars reflected in the ripples below. The mosquitoes would be after her soon. She had noticed a
pattern each evening; the sun went down, then
the wind dropped, and then came the pests.
Only this time another pest was out before the
winged kind.

"Stargazing?" Tony asked from behind her,
using his velvet voice most effectively.

Kate had not heard his arrival in the soft sand
and she turned and gazed at him warily, wishing she had not been quite so obvious in her
choice of a stopping place. "No, just needing a
few minutes alone. I run out of steam about this
time every day and it takes being completely by
myself to restore my batteries." If it was a little
blunt, then so be it. Tony, unfortunately, had
shown himself all but impervious to subtle
hints.

"It does get a bit much, doesn't it?" he agreed,
leaning over the rail beside her. "Those old
biddies in the room across the hall go on half the
night. Besides, I can think of better ways to
spend my nights than bunked in with a bunch of
snoring old men."

"Sorry about that. You could have put up at a
motel, you know. Boarding in wasn't compul-
sory."

"Oh, it's not the sharing I mind, Katie, love—
it's the choice of roommates. Now, if we were to
do it all over again, I'd insist on choosing my
own." He nudged her shoulder and picked up
one of her hands, playing idly with her fingers
before she snatched them away.

"Not now, Tony, please. I'm not in the mood for one of your verbal passes." She moved away and tried to ignore him, hoping he'd take the hint.

"Then we'll move on to the action," he said, snaking an arm around her and pulling her half off balance. "Maybe I've been missing your signals and it's more than pretty speeches you're wanting. After all, your tame boyfriend has been gone over a week now and you could be having as much trouble sleeping as I am." Before she could escape, he was pulling her against him, overcoming her resistance with a surprisingly wiry strength. When he crushed her arms against his chest and buried his face in her throat, his deep laugh bringing shudders of revulsion to her, she raged, "You're disgusting! Tony, stop it!"

"Come on, honey, don't be like that. You haven't had any loving since Brookwood left and you must be as hungry as I am."

She kicked at him and lost her balance and he took advantage of her momentary weakness to cover her mouth with his hot, eager lips. Finally, knowing herself outmatched, she decided to cool his ardor by remaining completely impassive. If he thought he was irresistible, that ought to prick his egotistical balloon!

The kiss went on and on and she felt her stomach churning. There was nothing more repulsive than being mauled by someone you didn't care for and Tony Palani had rapidly descended from someone she barely tolerated to someone she actively despised. She was still standing frozen in his disgusting embrace when the headlights swept around the curve to the

bridge approach and Tony's face left hers in
time for her to see the gunmetal Mercedes as it
passed within a foot of where they were standing.

Cameron was at the wheel, of course, his face
a sneering mask in the dim interior lighting, and
unmistakably silhouetted beside him was Stella
Wright.

The day of the open house began with showers
and cleared beautifully just before lunch. They
had chipped in and bought the makings for
punch, and Selma and Gretchen had popped
gallons of popcorn and cubed pounds of cheese
to go with the assortment of crackers.

The paintings were only matted, of course, but
in spite of that they looked surprisingly good. By
careful selection, it had been possible to include
several from each student without detracting
seriously from the quality of the exhibit, and
everyone was in a cheerful mood.

Everyone except Tony, that was. He was still
sulking after having struck out the night before.
It must have done irreparable harm to his
fragile macho image to have the two women he
had selected for his attentions both reject him.
When Stella wandered in when the afternoon
was half over, he gave her a look that could have
ignited paper.

More guests showed up than Kate had dared
hope and there were even a few sales to brighten
spirits. Of course, the prices were ridiculously
low, but then, the buyers were getting one-of-a-
kind original art and who knew which of the
painters would go on to become well known. At
about four-thirty, Kate sensed attention pull

away from the exhibit and the refreshment table and she leaned over to where she could see the front door. Cameron stood there, his hand on Dotty's shoulder, and he surveyed the room coolly.

Dotty hurried over and spoke to several of the students she had met during the course of the past two weeks, but Cameron remained aloof, looking down his aristocratic nose at the lot of them, Kate decided indignantly. She watched him saunter slowly into the room, his hands in the pockets of his flawlessly tailored cream-colored slacks and wondered in spite of herself how such a mean, hateful soul could be housed in such a magnificent body.

"It's delightful, Kate," Dotty exclaimed, coming up to her with a cup of punch in her bejeweled hand. "The show, I mean, although this punch isn't half bad. What is it, anyway?"

"Nothing you'd ever recognize, Dotty," Kate laughed. "Just a mixture of what was available, I'm afraid. You have to offer something at these affairs, unfortunately, besides art, otherwise folks stay away in great droves."

"You seem to know how to put it together."

"I've done the school shows for four years now," Kate told the older woman, "and, of course, I've been to every type opening there is, from the caviar and imported champagne sort to the ones where they drop Alka-Seltzer into cheap sauterne and assume a haughty look."

They laughed together. Dotty expressed an interest in one of the watercolors of Bay Oaks, and then Stella and Tony converged on them from opposite sides of the room. Tony was obviously under the influence of something

more than the innocent punch and Kate braced
herself for unpleasantness.

"Hello, Dotty," Stella drawled. "Haven't seen
you around lately."

"No, but then I try to stay out of the way
whenever Cam has a heavy load of work to get
done. It's so important in his line to have
undisturbed peace and quiet, you know," Dotty
answered smoothly, her small, snapping eyes
half hidden in their bed of wrinkles.

Stella shrugged off the innuendo, if, indeed, it
were one, and sniffed when Tony draped an arm
across Kate's shoulder. "A little undisturbed
peace and quiet's what we're all looking for,
isn't it, Katie, darling, but then, the way Kate's
had to push lately, the only time we can find to
be alone is after the thundering herd turns in,"
he said fatuously.

Kate could cheerfully have throttled him. She
tried to remove herself from under his arm
without making a federal case of it, not trusting
him one bit in this maliciously playful mood.
But when she stepped back, she cannoned into
something warm and hard, and she looked over
her shoulder to apologize and found herself
entangled in Cameron's tawny, disparaging
eyes.

Before either one of them could speak, Tony
continued, oblivious to any undertones in the
small group. "Did I tell you, Stell, that I've
decided to stay over for the next session?"

Kate gasped at this. "But you can't! It's all
filled!"

"Oh, no, it's not. Did I forget to give you the
message?" He looked at her in mock consternation. "Sorry, sweetheart. Greyville told me but I

clean forgot. Looks as if I can't be trusted, doesn't it?" He leered at his own double entendre.

"What the devil are you talking about, Tony? Speak up! If you know something I don't, then quit acting like a nasty little brat and tell me!" She should have known better, but her temper got the upper hand, and Tony's arm tightened on her shoulder until she thought her bones would crack. She'd like to shelve it for a more private occasion but there was nothing for it now but to plow on. At least there was safety in numbers, although at this moment she wasn't sure who was in the most danger—Tony or herself. "What message?" she asked again, weariness as well as wariness revealed in her voice.

"The kid from Richmond won't be coming. He had to go to the hospital for an emergency appendectomy, and that's a refundable cause for dropping out, if I remember correctly, so I've decided to do you a favor and stay on. My money's as good as the next man's, and besides, I'm already settled in—and loving every minute of it, I might add," he finished with a sickening leer.

Kate would have given twice the tuition just to wipe that look off his smoothly handsome face and she was determined to have it out with him, but not here, not in front of an all-too-avid audience. She couldn't help but be aware of the other two women as she stood there in Tony's casual-appearing embrace. Stella looked knowingly amused and Kate was half convinced that the whole thing was done in order to get back at her for rejecting him—to get back at both of them, for that matter.

Dotty looked sympathetic enough, but she was unable to keep that slightly wicked look of speculation from her eyes, and Kate was fast coming to realize that Dotty Greyville was not above tossing the cat among the pigeons in order to stir up a little entertainment.

Only Cameron's reaction was hidden from her, and not for all the tea in China would she have turned around to face him. As it was, she fancied she could feel the heat emanating from his body close behind her and so she was doubly shocked when she heard the front screen door slam and saw him stride past the window on his way back to Bay Oaks.

Chapter Three

True to his threat, Tony stayed on, and Kate could come up with no real grounds for turning him away. It was true, she did need the money, for she had budgeted very carefully, spending all she could afford on advertising in a national art magazine and brochures to follow up inquiries with, as well as on the lease itself. Annie's salary was saved, of course, but she had not counted on the high cost of the meals, for everyone's appetites seemed to have tripled in the salt air.

Tony's staying also meant that she did not have the two-day respite between sessions in which to shore up her sagging energies. Everyone was packed and gone by nine on Saturday morning and she had counted on having a quiet little break before the next group came trailing

in late Sunday afternoon. Instead, Tony insisted
on taking her sight-seeing and she found herself
agreeing weakly against her own inclination.
Maybe she was more tired than she thought.
Teaching took the starch out of her, especially
since she was conducting two sessions a day of
two-and-a-half-hour duration, plus the after-
dinner critique-demonstration, and it was impossible to turn them off like a faucet at the end
of any class. There were always questions, and
they inevitably led to discussions, and, as often
as not, she found one class running directly into
the other without her having taken time for
lunch.

There was that, too. In spite of an enthusiastic
promise on the part of her students to see to the
chores and the cooking, Kate was invariably the
one who ended up putting together meals and
cleaning up afterward. The days were growing
increasingly hot and humid, too.

They saw the Hatteras Lighthouse, as well as
the tragic remains of the old one that had been
destroyed during the War Between the States
and was now only a few huge stones at the edge
of the hungry Atlantic Ocean. They visited the
nearby museum and walked the nature trail,
swatting mosquitoes as they read the informa-
tive signs along the way. Tony's driving left her
clutching the bucket seat of the dashing red
Aston Martin, but she knew instinctively that if
she mentioned it it would only egg him on. As
ingratiating as he was acting at the moment,
there was something about Tony Palani that set
Kate's nerves on edge, and she would be glad to
see the last of him.

They ate in one of the better restaurants on

Saturday night, after dropping off the huge load of laundry, and Kate had to admit it was nice to enjoy a meal she hadn't prepared. They had reached the dessert stage—not that Kate could have eaten another bite—when Cameron and Dotty walked in. Dotty saw them immediately and led her grandson across the room to their waterfront table, ignoring the frown on Tony's face as she greeted Kate warmly.

"Won't you join us?" Tony asked, the words obviously forced from him reluctantly.

"Oh, but you're just finishing," Dotty protested unconvincingly.

"Nonsense," Cameron insisted, drawing up a chair for his grandmother and another for himself. "I'm sure they'll enjoy another coffee and we'll have the advantage of a good table, not that there's much of a crowd at this hour." He looked lean and handsome and somehow pleased with himself, and it occurred to Kate that a man of his nature could be infinitely dangerous.

Dotty chattered on while their order was taken and there didn't seem to be an opening to leave. Kate could tell Tony was restless, but she was eager to hear all about Dotty's latest project of encasing wild flowers in acrylic in a variety of molds. The fact that Cameron's imposing figure was only inches away had nothing to do with it, and she was hard put to account for her breathlessness when his leg inadvertently encountered her own under the table.

They parted finally, with the excuse of having to collect the laundry plus a few groceries, and it did not occur to Kate until they were on their way back to Coranoke that tonight she would be all alone in the house with Tony. She felt suddenly terribly vulnerable, especially since Tony's attitude seemed to have deteriorated since they had finished their own dinner. Maybe it hadn't been such a good idea to subject him to almost an hour of Dotty's prattle, but they had had little enough else to do, and it was pleasant in the restaurant—as much of a break as Kate had allowed herself in some time.

They pulled up in front of the house and she sat there, reluctant to face the next step. "I'll get the laundry and you can carry the groceries," she said finally.

"Are you asking or telling?"

"I'm asking, but it wouldn't hurt you to offer. You certainly consume your share of them." Not very gracious after his having taken her out, but she couldn't help it.

"Seeing as how I'm paying through the nose for it, I wouldn't complain if I were you," he came back.

"You know, Tony, you're really not a particulary nice person, are you?" She had the unsettling feeling he was about to demand more than an art lesson for his money and she was thinking frantically of a way to fend him off.

"Once you get to know me better, you're going to love me," he told her with a crooked smile. "I'm not a stingy sort, either. I can be very generous under the right circumstances." He reached for her and she scuttled away, her hand on the door latch.

"You're disgusting! I think you'd better take off, Tony. You haven't paid anything for the second term and all of a sudden I find it necessary to limit the enrollment." She was out of the car and reaching for the boxes in the back when he caught her and she slapped out at him angrily. She should have handled it better, she supposed, but who expects to be attacked while they're unloading groceries? "Tony, behave yourself!"

He had come around the car so swiftly that he caught her completely by surprise, his arms going around her waist from behind so that she was unable to straighten up. She tried kicking, but it didn't work and she resorted to profanity, a skill that she had never perfected.

"Calm down, sweetheart. You know you've been counting the hours today just like I have. I thought that old windbag was never going to let us go, but it's you and me now, baby, and you're about to find out what a lucky gal you are." He lifted her by the shoulders and turned her to face him in spite of her protests and she swung at him just as the headlights appeared and bathed them in a blinding spotlight for an instant.

"Oh, good Lord, Tony, am I going to have to call the sheriff?" she exploded angrily, furious at being caught brawling in such an undignified manner by the car that had driven up the oleander-lined driveway of Bay Oaks and stopped.

"What would you charge me with? I haven't done anything that you haven't been inviting me to do for weeks, have I? Women like to play their little games—lead 'em on, push 'em back—but I've got a few games in mind, too, honey, and I guarantee you're gonna love 'em."

"You're an utter swine!" she yelled at him, jerking herself from his grasp. She turned and began to run, not caring about the laundry, the groceries, or anything except getting away from those greedy, clutching hands. Unfortunately, she had miscalculated the enemy, and when he put out a foot, she went sprawling headlong in the sand.

"They all fall for me sooner or later," Tony quipped facetiously, leaning over to lift her up, but she drew herself up into a defensive ball and kicked out at him.

"Go away, will you? Just leave me alone!" There were tears of pure rage burning her eyes and she was more frightened than she dare let on.

"You heard what she said. Get!" came a familiar gravelly baritone, and Kate clenched her fists in frustration. Was it utterly inevitable that Cam should be witness to every mortifying encounter she had with Tony Palani?

She felt herself being lifted up from under her arms as if she weren't five feet six inches of solid flesh and then Cameron was brushing the hair from her face and inquiring with a rough sort of tenderness if she were all right.

"Well, of course I'm all right! What did you expect!" Embarrassment made her sound so shrewish she could have kicked herself.

Cameron's hands dropped from her shoulders to her upper arms and any possible tenderness he might have revealed a moment ago was gone as they bit into her soft skin. "If I'd expected a little common politeness I'd have been damned disappointed! Go on in to your little friend! I guess I just made a mistake all around! His money is as good as the next man's after all," he sneered, and turned away to go.

"Wait!"

He looked back over his shoulder, contempt and disinterest written on his face.

"I'm sorry," she gritted out, struggling to keep her voice level. Then, as a flood of tension drained away, leaving her limp and shaken: "I'm really sorry. And—and I do thank you, Mr. Greyville. I don't know what I would have done. Well, of course, I could have handled the situation, but even so—"

"Handled the situation! Don't be any more a fool than you can help, you stupid woman! If you could have handled the situation, I wouldn't have had to intervene. If you had even a grain of sense, you'd never have put yourself in that position in the first place!"

"Oh, great! Thank you for those words of wisdom, Mr. Greyville!" she blurted out a little wildly. "Just think, if the whole world knew what you know, no one would ever get themselves in trouble ever again!"

"You and that mob of yours! I ought to leave you to paddle yourself out of the muck you've landed in, you and that flock of posturing, chattering magpies! Just tell them to keep away from my side of the island!" He was towering over her again and she unconsciously stretched herself up to her inadequate tallest, thrusting out her chin belligerently.

"You don't seem to object to at least one of my posturing, chattering magpies," she told him with mock sweetness. "I notice that as soon as your little top-ten tootsie moved out, you didn't waste any time filling the vacancy with Stella Wright. Too bad she had to leave, too."

"Too bad is right. At least she knew how to behave like a woman instead of a frustrated, bad-tempered shrew who . . ."

He wasn't allowed to finish. Kate swung wildly and Cameron stood with mocking insolence and took the blow squarely on the cheek. Then, as she watched in shock, he reached out and jerked her against him with a punishing force that rattled her teeth. His mouth came down on her outraged protest and she seethed with impotent fury as his hands began to move over her body with an insulting thoroughness. She twisted and kicked out and he only tightened his hold, bringing her into shocking proximity to his angry, aroused body, and when the kiss changed imperceptibly into something less aggressive and more subtly seductive, she found her anger unaccountably draining away. It was then that his kiss broke the barrier of her determination and invaded the warm, soft depths of her.

By the time he had finished with her, Kate was shaking from the reaction, and he put her away from him abruptly, retaining the grip on her shoulders for an agonizing moment before turning her in the direction of Bay Oaks. "Go and tell Dotty to pour you a stiff drink," he ordered peremptorily.

Mindlessly, she had already taken half a dozen steps before she came to her senses. "I can't do that! The groceries . . . Tony—I don't even know where he is."

"I'll take care of all that. Now go and do as I said—unless you're anxious to join Palani. He's still inside nursing his jaw, if you're feeling sympathetic," he sneered. The challenge was unmistakable, but Kate was in no condition to meet it, and she turned with unaccustomed meekness and stumbled across the sandy stretch that separated the two houses.

Cameron returned some twenty minutes later and, without speaking to either of the two women in the room, poured himself a stiff drink and tossed it back. Then he poured another and crossed to a large pine and leather chair, and only then did he level a look at Kate. "You're welcome to stay the night if you'd care to, but Palani won't be bothering you anymore, I can assure you."

Kate was stunned to realize that she wanted nothing so much as to snuggle into the comfort of this rambling house and forget all about her classes, forget Tony and the stack of linens to be put away and the groceries melting in their boxes and everything except for the unqualified friendliness of the old woman and the strength that emanated from Cameron Greyville in a palpable aura.

Feeling oddly more threatened now than ever before, she made herself stand and place her glass carefully on the drop-leaf table. "In that case, I can only thank you, but I'll go along now. He . . . it was just that Tony caught me off guard," she prevaricated. "As a rule I'm more than competent to handle . . . that sort of thing." She felt drained, washed out, and for once the flood of warmth that arose in her face gave her the added strength she needed to escape with at least a few tattered remnants of her pride intact. She had told Dotty only what she had to, considering the other woman had seen the initial attack, but Cameron—that man had a way of dissecting her very emotions with surgical thoroughness, laying her bare to his withering examination!

"Thank you again," she blurted, hurrying to the door before either of them could rise, and she didn't stop running until she was at her own door.

Tony's car was gone and somehow it came as no surprise to find all his belongings missing. There was a sort of hollowness about the old house that echoed her own solitary emptiness as she walked slowly through the rooms, not really conscious of anything except for a weary sort of relief at his going.

She came at last to the kitchen to find the boxes from the grocery store stacked neatly on the table, and there beside them, weighted down with the clamshell ashtray, was a stack of bills. Numbly, she fingered them, then started through the stack again and counted. It amounted to exactly the sum of room, board, and tuition for a two-week session.

But Tony had already paid for his first course and surely he wouldn't leave money for a class he wouldn't be taking. Would he? Was it perhaps a guilty conscience that had made him leave the cash for her to find? She shrugged. He was gone now, and there was nothing that could be done about it tonight. She'd mail it to him in a day or so. She didn't want anything of his under any circumstances!

The next morning Kate was awakened by a sound that at first she couldn't identify. It was all mixed up with the dream she had been having, a dream that faded with the coming of daylight, and she lay there, blinking awake,

wondering why she felt so reluctant to get up.
The door opened and Cameron Greyville stood
there.

"Are you absolutely insane?" she demanded in
a dazed tone, sitting up with a total unaware-
ness of how she must look in her thin white
nightgown, her dark brown hair tumbling in
thick waves over her tanned shoulders.

"I knocked—both outside and on your own
door—but when there was no answer, I was
afraid—well, I can see that you're all right
now."

"Get out of here!"

"I want to speak to you. Now, before Dotty gets
here."

"Look, have you any idea what time it is? This
is no time for morning calls, so whatever
you . . ."

"Pipe down!" He crossed the room in two
strides and seated himself at the foot of her bed
and Kate drew the cotton bedspread up under
her chin.

"You play a marvelous outraged virgin, my
dear, but that's not what I've got on my mind at
the moment." His eyes dropped to roam her
clearly outlined form beneath the light covers
before returning to her sleep-flushed face.
"Dotty has a bee in her bonnet about taking your
course. With Palani gone, there's a vacancy."

"So?" she demanded suspiciously.

"So . . . let her come, let her play along and
don't be too critical of her efforts. I want her to
enjoy herself without worrying too much about
coming up to your standards, if you have any, do
you understand?"

"In spite of your insinuation, Mr. Greyville, I

do have standards and I'm sure Dotty will fit comfortably in the class. I happen to like *her* very much, surprisingly enough."

"The inference being that you find her grandson slightly less palatable," he returned in a soft jeer.

"Exactly!"

"You know, Miss Brown, I find it remarkable that two males in the past two weeks have been willing to risk your thorns in search of any possible nectar," he mused.

"My love life, Mr. Greyville, is my own affair!" Kate retorted, forgetting the covers entirely as her fists clenched impotently at her sides.

As if she hadn't spoken, he went on. "But then, maybe you haven't met the right type yet. I understand even the most thorny plants are open to pollination when the right insect comes along."

"If you're through with your little lecture on horticulture, Mr. Greyville, perhaps you'd kindly get out of my bedroom!"

His finger traced her leg hidden under the covers from knee to ankle and then it circled about her foot and squeezed it gently. "I thought I was talking about the birds and the bees, Katydid." He grinned infuriatingly. The light from her window was dancing across his broad shoulders, making patterns on the clinging knit shirt, and she made a strangled sound as she jerked her foot away from him.

"For your information, Cameron Greyville, I find men remarkably easy to do without altogether. They're a bunch of pompous, opinionated, overstuffed, bullying, arrogant . . . !"

"Don't choke on your own wrath, Kate, darling. I suspect you're throwing out a Freudian challenge."

"Get out!" she raged.

"If I get too bored this summer, I might even take you up on it," he promised, his parting shot delivered just before he closed the door after himself.

The second session began smoothly with a more or less harmonious group. It was a younger group, on the whole, with a social worker, a kindergarten teacher, two housewives, a retired minister, and two jaded-looking men who told her they were on sabbatical in order to "find themselves." Dotty was a delight to have. She showed up that first morning with no material, but before the class was half over Cameron drove up to where they were located, just on the Hatteras side of the bridge, and dropped off enough to send her through a year of art school.

Kate was chagrined to find herself musing on the tenderness he showed his grandmother and she turned to the minister, Mr. Backlighter, and began instructing him vigorously on the laying of a graded wash, suggesting that he turn his paper upside down to insure an even flow from the horizon to the zenith. By the time she had finished explaining what she meant, Cameron had driven off again.

Which was, of course, a great relief!

By midweek the rains came. It had been unseasonably dry, to the point where there was a forest fire watch on the mainland, and park rangers were being particularly strict with campers. Dotty, coming over for the evening session after dinner, invited the class to assemble on one or the other of the porches at Bay Oaks the next morning.

"Dotty, I appreciate it, but I don't think your grandson would care for the idea. I've more or less had my orders about where I'm not to trespass," Kate said.

"Cam? Why, I'm sure you must have misunderstood him, dear. My goodness, Cam was the one who suggested that I join your class in the first place, although I'd probably not have been able to resist anyway. You all looked as if you were having such a ball over across the bridge, and all I could do here was listen to Cam muttering about phase-shift and resonance and try to keep those hussies off his neck."

She paid her tuition that night, although Kate tried to refuse. She had mailed back the money Tony left without bothering to write a note. He'd understand. Even he was not so insensitive as all that! Now, with the smaller payment from Dotty, she felt as if she were beginning to get her head above water.

Protecting themselves with a variety of headgear—mostly plastic bags—the class trouped across the wet sand at nine thirty on the dot the next morning. She tried to allow fifteen minutes for them to get set up and settled down, although there were always a few who used every minute to the best advantage. The young social worker was that sort, and he was turning out to be a first-rate watercolorist. Kate reminded herself to speak to him about exhibiting opportunities before he left.

Cameron didn't show himself and for that Kate was heartily glad. She had not seen him since that morning when he barged into her bedroom and if she never saw him again it would be too soon! At least that's what she told herself whenever his aggravating image came between her and whatever she was trying to concentrate on. It simply wasn't fair that he should persist in haunting her when she did her best to avoid him. Damn his virile body and his handsome, mocking face!

The rain lasted four days and by the time it ended Kate felt as if she'd been walking a tightrope of naked nerves. It was not that they weren't a great group—they were. It was a joy to teach them. But there was something unsettling about a high-ceilinged house without the softening effects of rugs, draperies, and upholstered furniture. Every noise was magnified until her nerves were jangled unbearably. Even music was beginning to make her jumpy, and when one of the younger members of the class brought out a guitar after the evening session and they all settled down to what promised to be a long, noisy evening, she had to escape. She slipped out the back door unnoticed and followed the moonlit path down to the wharf.

The air was redolent of gardenias from the row of flowering shrubs that lined the drive to Bay Oaks. Cape Jasmines, Dotty called them, but whatever the name, the effect was the same—lethal to any edging-into-middle-aged spinster who found herself alone on a moonlit island. She remembered a book she had laughed over with several of the other teachers. It had been a Victorian volume of advice to young ladies entering the so-called dangerous years. "When the python rears its ugly head, play basketball, girls, play basketball!"

Much more of this moonlight and gardenias and she'd have to see about getting herself some sports equipment.

It was the first time she had been near the wharf since that first day when Cameron had rescued her from Pelican Shoal and returned her ignominiously to Hal Brookwood. Now, with a three-quarter moon riding high over a few tentative wisps of cloud, it looked completely different. With a landscape painter's insight, she noted the refraction of moonlight on the mist that hovered just above the surface of the water and allowed her fantasies full play. In her mind's eye, the salt-bleached pilings that arose from the misty water might have been columns of marble and the moon-white roofs that showed above the shadowy, wind-sculpted trees over on Hatteras could well have been a ruined city on some distant continent.

In her bemused state, she had no warning of any intrusion and her heart leapt up suffocatingly when someone spoke from immediately behind her. She twisted around to see Cameron Greyville towering over her and immediately all the old antagonism flared into life. Almost as immediately, it fizzled like a damp match and went out. The combination of mist, moonlight, and muffled water music would not support the combustion.

Cameron dropped lightly down beside her, his feet, like hers, dangling over the edge of the weathered wharf. Kate hooked a toe under the mooring line of the skiff and moved it silently back and forth, and neither of them spoke until Cameron lifted a hand to swat a mosquito. "It takes nerve to brave these dive bombers. What brought you out here tonight?"

"The promise of a few minutes of solid, twenty-four karat silence. I'd forgotten just how noisy old houses can be when they don't have much furniture in them to muffle the sound."

"I remember. When I was about, oh, nine or ten years old, we lived in an old Victorian relic. The day before we moved, after everything was packed and stacked, my brother and I spent the entire day whispering to each other from the third floor to the first," Cameron told her.

"I didn't know you had a brother." What a silly thing to say! Why *should* she know anything about his family?

"He was killed in a fall on Drakensberg."

The stark words fell oddly on her ears, as if it weren't a real human being they were discussing. Somehow she couldn't believe Cameron was that cool and unfeeling—not after seeing him with Dotty. "I'm sorry," she murmured after a slight pause.

After a still longer pause—one that was filled with the buzz of insects, the slapping of the water against the bottom of the boats, and the distant sound of music—he said, "It was four years ago. We hadn't seen all that much of each other since he married, but the closeness was still there."

What could one say? "I'm sorry," she repeated. "It must have been dreadful for his wife. He couldn't have been very old."

He looked down at her then. Before, they had both been watching the intermittent blink of the channel lights. "He was thirty-six—the same

age I am now. As for Barbara, she only waited
long enough for the estate to be settled before
she married into a diamond mine in South
Africa."

The words were so dispassionate that there
was really nothing she could say. She rejected
the implication, and after another long but not
uncomfortable silence she told him how much
she was enjoying having Dotty in her class.
"You've no idea how much fun she is," she went
on. "I've never seen anyone throw themselves
into a project with such abandon, and for someone her age, it's doubly remarkable."

"Oh, I've a pretty good idea of how much fun
Dotty is. We've been together for a long time
now, she and I, and she's given me a good deal
of pleasure." He smiled and Kate caught it from
the sidelong glance she gave him, conscious of
the increased rate of her pulse. "She claimed to
be fifty-nine for almost a decade, and when Ivor
and I used to tease her about being only nine
years older than her son, she told us it was the
new math."

They laughed softly, easily, and Kate was
astounded at how pleasant it was to be sitting
here with him. Cameron told her to be still, that
there was a mosquito aiming for her jugular,
and then his hand touched her and the mosquito
was forgotten. Tension built into a shimmering,
brittle thing as his hand moved hypnotically,
stroking and soothing the skin of her throat and
her shoulder. Slowly, her movements weighted
with a druglike heaviness, she turned to look up
at him, and when his face came down on hers,
her lips were already parted.

Somehow they found themselves lying back on the satiny boards—boards still warm from the day's sun—and Cameron cradled her in one arm as the other one drew her compellingly close to his vital body. He kissed her with a thoroughness that suggested that there was all the time in the world, his mouth playing teasing games with her hungry lips until she lifted a hand and touched the back of his head, holding him there, afraid of a world that didn't contain his nearness.

"Did you know your eyes are the color of Spanish moss after a rain? I can see the color even here at night," Cameron murmured, one finger trailing over her brows, down her cheek, to the corner of her mouth, and then, with relentless gentleness, down her throat to climb the soft mound of her breast.

It was impossible to hide her reaction from him and his finger trailed tantalizing circles around the rapidly hardening peak as he continued to smile maddeningly into her eyes. Her breath was a fluttering gasp as Cameron deliberately tormented her to the point of insensibility, and then, when she was utterly helpless, he lowered his head again to claim the freely offered open flower of her mouth, teasing, suggesting, seducing her senses as his hands traced lightly across her breasts, triggering off all sorts of wild, impossible longings. When they strayed to her waist and splayed out over her stomach, she stiffened and caught at them, and he lifted his face easily, desisting as if it mattered not at all to him.

"Wel-l-l," he breathed softly, fanning her face

with warmth after endless moments of cart-
wheeling through the night. "An unexpected
source of honey."

The word association was unfortunate, taking
Kate back to the time when he had remarked on
thorns encountered in a search for nectar, and
she stiffened away from him.

"Second thoughts already, Katie?" He traced a
fine line down the narrow bridge of her nose,
dropping his finger to her lips, still moist from
his kisses, and she panicked.

"Leave me alone. I . . . I want to go inside
now."

"No one's stopping you, Katie, if you want to
run away. It occurred to me that the evening
might be incomplete without a little light lovemaking, but if you're satisfied with moonlight
and polite conversation, that's all right by me.
No big loss."

She scrambled to her feet with more haste
than dignity and backed away from him, turning
blindly and hurrying toward the house lights
that reached out to meet her. Her throat was
aching before she had gone halfway and she
wondered frantically what had happened to her
levelheadedness. The first nonaggressive word
from him and she fell into his arms like a
lovesick adolescent! "No big loss," he had said,
and she dare not think of the loss that threatened her now.

The weather cleared enough so that they could
go further afield, thankfully, and the term ended
without any further contact with Cameron Greyville. Dotty didn't mention his name and Kate

wasn't about to bring it up, although she couldn't avoid casting an occasional glance in the direction of Bay Oaks.

The second exhibit was an unqualified success and several of the villagers remarked that they were looking forward to the next one. Kate found them unexpectedly enthusiastic, and when the woman who had bought a watercolor from the first show mentioned signing up for one of the later courses, she found herself making room for three more without once recalling her determination to limit the size of her classes. By the end of the summer, their plans might have changed anyhow, or someone might drop out again, but now, in the euphoric mood of a successful afternoon, she agreed to almost everything that was suggested to her.

Everyone left the next morning and Kate went back to bed, nursing a headache she put down to the persistent southeast winds. Her eyelids felt thick and her fingers were stiff on awakening and she sneezed twice before she got up grumpily and made herself a pot of coffee. She couldn't sleep any better in the echoing silence of the empty house than she had been able to with all the whisperings, the coughs and rustlings, and when she heard Cam's car leave the garage she emptied the dregs of her second cup down the drain, unconsciously straightened her shoulders, and went in and put on her best sun dress, topping it off with a bright slash of Midas Red lipstick for good measure.

This time she had allowed herself more than just the two half-days between sessions. It had occurred to her while she was making out her schedule back in November that she owed herself a full week every month and now she was glad she had. She needed every single minute of it if she were to give each group what they deserved.

On her second free morning Dotty came around just before lunch and suggested that they go out for a seafood salad. Kate was only too glad of any excuse to leave Coranoke, for in spite of her best efforts, she had been dragging around the house, unable to settle to anything. Not even a note from Iola calling her attention to a clipping that she had forgotten to enclose lifted her spirits for long.

They went to a restaurant further up the beach and Kate, in a mood of defiance, ordered the most expensive seafood salad on the menu and then was chagrined to find her appetite had deserted her. Her embarrassment was doubled when Dotty insisted on paying, clinching the argument with the irrefutable statement that she was determined not to leave it behind, if she couldn't take it with her, and her friends had an obligation to help her spend it while she was still here to enjoy it.

They stopped at a gift shop on the way home and Kate bought small, locally made craft items for France and Iola. France's last letter—a hasty, impatient scrawl—had left her with a niggling feeling of disquiet, expressing, as it had, her sister's decision to go to England as much before the actual auditions as possible in order to find her feet on a strange continent. She had expressed dissatisfaction with her job, which she said was dull, dull, dull! and was of the opinion that it really wasn't worth the wear and tear on her sensitive nature.

Some of this Kate mentioned to Dotty as they drove through Frisco. Kate had taken her own car, for Dotty admitted to having surrendered her license two years before. "I'm healthy as a horse and my eyes aren't a day older than twenty-five—well, maybe thirty-five—and I've got a constitution like a billygoat, so the darned fools wouldn't pull my license. Purely for the sake of my own neck, I had to turn it in, Kate. I like speed, you see . . . love to feel the accelerator shoving the floorboards—always did! Lately, though, I've decided I'd rather hang around for a few more years before going back for recycling."

When they got back to Bay Oaks, Dotty invited Kate to come inside for a drink, but Kate declined. Cameron might or might not be home, but she could do without another confrontation.

"Then come on and let me show you my favorite of all the spots on the island. You look to me as if you could do with a taste of my own special recipe for relaxation."

Curiosity led Kate to accompany her to the other side of the island—a matter of several hundred yards—and then they dropped down an eroded, sandy bank, using one of the overhanging scrub oak branches for a handhold. They were on a shallow, hard-packed, sandy beach, with huge mounds of seaweed looking like soft, brown excelsior blown into moon crater shapes. Dotty explained that the winter seas heaped it up onto the sheltered beach and then high tides and strong winds left it in cratered, pillowy piles, perfect for lounging about in.

"Try it! It's absolute heaven, once you get used to the smell of iodine and salt. Pick out a heap that looks about your size and flop down on it, soak up some of the sun and breathe this air. Make a new woman of you, and frankly, Kate, you look lately as if you'd been pulled through a thicket backwards."

An hour later, Kate had to agree with her as to the efficacy of dozing on a dreamy, if unorthodox mattress with only the sounds of lapping water, rustling leaves, and the distant cry of the sea birds to lull her into dropping all her defenses. The sun beat down on her and she inhaled the scent of a million tiny sea creatures in various states of decomposition, and some strange, spicy, woodsy smell, and the combination was not at all unpleasant—rather exotic, really.

She was in that delicious state of creative awareness that comes between sleep and wakefulness when she became conscious of still another sound. Someone was whistling softly nearby. She opened her eyes, and for a moment she could see nothing but the shadowy, wooded bank above her. Then she focused closer and saw Cameron, his knees bent and his feet braced on the edges, lying flat on his back in the center of the cratered mound next to her. She watched him without speaking for several minutes, safe in the knowledge that he could not see her from that angle, for his head was in her direction, and she saw for the first time the slight scattering of silver in his dark blond hair. His muscular thighs were parted, their long, lithe strength emphasized by the faded jeans he wore, and the arms that were crossed under his head were tanned under their covering of dark hair, and exceptionally well formed. Her artist's eye noted the beauty almost impersonally before moving on to study his slender, but powerful-looking hands.

"Decided to rejoin the living?" he asked laconically when she had been studying him for several minutes.

"How did you know I was awake?"

"Felt those lovely eyes of yours boring through the top of my head."

"The cynosure of all eyes. Pretty self-conscious, aren't you?" she jeered, not unkindly.

"I wouldn't exactly choose those words, but yes, I'm aware of myself. Aren't you?"

To herself, she admitted that she was, and never more so than when in the company of Cameron Greyville. "No more than anyone else," she allowed.

He turned around and resettled himself so that he was facing her. This time, instead of lying back, he remained sitting upright, taking one of her feet in his hand and examining it carefully. She had left her shoes up on the bank and now she wished she hadn't. The touch of his fingers on her bare sole was registering on a seismograph somewhere in the pit of her stomach.

"Size six, right?" he grinned lazily.

"You sound pretty experienced when it comes to women's shoe sizes."

"And you're thinking that I'd be even more experienced when it came to other articles of apparel, right?"

She shrugged, or as much as she could in

her reclining position. "If the shoe fits . . . No pun intended." And then, when he didn't reply, she was tempted into indiscretion. "Are you?"

"You mean, have I ever bought an article of apparel for a lady? I take it you're not interested in anything I might buy for Dotty?"

"I'm not interested in anything you ever bought for anyone. Period," she protested.

"Oh, but then you don't know what superb taste I have in lady's unmentionables. Quiet, understated—real lace, of course—and black's nice, although brown can be pretty fetching, too." The glint in his eyes was unmistakable and she snapped at him.

"Oh, shut up! I told you I wasn't interested and I meant it, although if you ask me, your little secretary would lean more to marabou and rhinestones!"

"Ha!" The exclamation was both triumphant and amused, and he dropped her foot and clasped her knee instead, pressing it until she was forced to sit up and glare at him. "You sound as if no man ever offered you anything more romantic than a subscription to *Washington Week*. Are you jealous, little Katie?"

"No, I'm not jealous! You can have all the tartlets you want, and I hope you get tooth decay and an upset stomach!"

"Don't be unkind, Katie, you're not the type— and don't lie to me, either," he gibed gently.

"Oh . . . blast! Now you've gone and spoiled it!"

"Spoiled what?" he asked in all innocence.

"Dotty showed me this place so that I could get

a little much-needed relaxation and then you come along and barge in where you aren't wanted!"

"In case you've forgotten, my dear Katie, it's my island. The very bed of dried eelgrass that's cuddling your delectable body belongs to me. Now stop falling apart just because a man is paying you some attention. You're really not all that bad looking . . . for a woman of your mature years."

"You can just go . . . to . . . to . . . !" she blazed at him, and when he threw back his head and roared, she scrambled to her feet and stormed across the hard-packed sand to the embankment, searching distraughtly for the proper handhold to pull herself up.

Cameron stood easily, an unfolding of superbly conditioned muscles and reflexes, and indicated the way up the bank. "Oh, I almost forgot the reason I came after you," he told her as he handed down her shoes and waited while she hopped about, shoving them on sandy feet. "You've a visitor."

"A visitor? Who?" she frowned, hoping against hope it was not Hal Brookwood. She had been as discouraging as she could short of outright rudeness the last time she had seen him, but he had left with a promise of another visit.

"Palani." He spat out the name. "He drove up after you left with Dotty and I sent him on his way, but he came back, and when he saw your car, there was nothing for it but to tell him I'd fetch you. I didn't want him coming on his own, considering the way you two parted." He looked at her intently, searching for something. "Kate? Are you sure you want to see him? I can get rid of him, you know."

She frowned. "He must have a pretty good reason for looking me up," she mused. "It won't hurt anything to see what it is, I suppose. And anyway, you have no right to interfere with my guests," she added with a return to her former irritation. She reached for the branch that overhung the bank and he covered her hand with his own.

"A truce with you never lasts, does it?"

She swung around to glare at him, and before she could pull away he had brought up his other hand to the back of her head and held it, making her captive for his demanding mouth. She shoved against his chest, making muffled protests, and he ignored them, ignored her fists as if they were match sticks as he pulled her hard against him so that she was instantly aware of every tensed, straining muscle.

The feel of him, still hot with sunshine, burned through the thin fabric of her dress until it blocked out all awareness of the world beyond that virile, aggressive body, and the scent of him filled her nostrils, inflaming her senses. He had drained all her resistance, and when one hand smoothed down her spine and shaped her hips, she moved to accommodate herself to him. Somehow her hands had found their way beneath his shirt and they pressed against the warm, satiny skin of his back, causing him to stiffen and groan.

"Oh, Kate . . . you don't know what you're doing to me."

She drew away, thoroughly shaken, and he let her go, retaining his hold on her upper arms as she struggled for composure. "Cam, I don't know what happened . . . I mean, I don't usually . . ."

"I know, sweet. You're not that kind of a girl," he mocked gently. "Look, Kate—there's more than one way to discharge a potentially dangerous buildup of energy. Fighting's one—this was another. We strike sparks off each other, that's all. Don't make too big a deal of it, hm?"

Unreasonably stung at his easy dismissal, she flung back her head. Every nerve in her body was swollen and throbbing painfully and he dismissed it as no big deal! Well, for him it was probably a standard reaction to finding himself alone with a female, but for her . . . "Oh, go . . . go play with your computers! I despise men who think all they have to do is smile at a woman and she's ready to jump into bed with them!"

"Oh, did you consider my smiles an invitation then?"

She had pushed aside his helping hand and pulled herself up the bank and was stalking across the knoll with her chin out and a militant sparkle in her eye, furiously aware that his easy stride was making her look ridiculous. "If you want to know what I think, Mr. Greyville, I think you simply have to have a simpering female in tow for the sake of your overweening masculine ego! First Bebe, then Stella, and now, in their absence, me! Well, I'm not interested! You bore me, Mr. Greyville, with your predictable masculine ploys, and if I have a choice between fighting or . . . or kissing, I'll take fighting every time!"

"To be finished off with a stamp of the foot and a 'So there,' too," he remarked infuriatingly. "Go on inside. I left your caller with Dotty and there's no telling what mischief she's been up to while we were out."

His answering quip had completely disarmed her, for she had a highly irreverent sense of humor, and now she grumbled, "Well, you wasted enough time delivering the message."

Cameron held the door open with an unrepentant grin. "Won't do him any harm to cool his ardor a bit."

She paused at the large framed mirror in the hallway to touch her hair. It was windblown and she combed it with fingers that were slightly unsteady, thankful that with her rich tan she didn't really need makeup. Brushing a strand of dried eelgrass from her shoulder, she moved away and saw Cam leaning indolently against the wall, obviously waiting for her. She glowered at him, but it was impossible to maintain her indignation in the face of his warm, wicked grin.

"Ready?"

"Ready."

They crossed the large, airy living room to the comfortable porch beyond and Kate smiled uncertainly at Tony. Dotty, a drink in her hand, was reclining on a cushioned chaise, and Tony was standing awkwardly in the middle of the room, as if he weren't quite sure of his welcome.

"Ah, there you are, Kate," Dotty exclaimed immediately. "I've been enjoying your visitor, my dear. Tony tells me he's come down to spend the rest of the week with you, but I warned him"—she shook a gnarled, bejeweled finger playfully—"that he'd have to compete with Cam for your time. Of course, we know it isn't official yet, but even so, you won't have as much time as you used to have, will you, dear?"

Chapter Four

Silence pulsated around them, suspending all action for an instant that seemed to stretch into eternity, and Kate saw Tony, his face a study in consternation, and Dotty, her bright eyes waiting for the explosion that should follow her outrageous remark, and Cameron, his own face enigmatic as he stepped up to her and raised a finger to her chin. Only then was she aware that her mouth was open and when he closed it gently, with a wink that no one could see except her, she pushed his hand away impatiently.

"Come now, dear, he has to know sometime," he told her composedly.

"Nobody has to . . ." she began, only to be shushed in no uncertain terms when Cam turned and asked Tony to please wait for them out front.

"Katie will be out in a minute. I daresay she's

upset because my grandmother jumped the gun instead of letting her break the news more tactfully, but then . . ." He shrugged, as if to say, "You know women," and Kate was even more furious when Tony, with a half-apologetic look, left the porch and vanished around the corner.

She turned first to Dotty. "That was unforgivable, Dotty. How could you?"

"Well, love, I was here with the young man for almost half an hour while Cam went to get you. What kept you, by the way?" she asked, with a parrot-bright gleam in her eyes. "He's a lecherous layabout, Katie. I know the type, believe me, and I wouldn't want to spend a night alone with him, so I thought fast and came up with the best protection I could at short notice. I knew Cam would go along with it," she pointed out with impossible insouciance.

"I'd rather take my chances with Tony—with Atilla the Hun, in fact—than be engaged to your grandson." It was shockingly ungracious, she knew, even as the words escaped her, for they were both only trying to protect her. All the same, Kate felt terribly vulnerable, and she threw up her defenses helter-skelter, repelling all boarders, so to speak.

"I wasn't aware that you'd been asked, Miss Brown," Cameron rejoined coolly, moving away from her to stand looking back toward the hidden beach they had so recently left.

"Oh, dear. I was going to invite you and Mr. Palani to have dinner with us tonight, Kate," Dotty said plaintively. "Does this mean you won't be coming now?"

Kate's eyes lifted heavenward while her fists

clenched impotently at her sides. The two of
them would be the death of her yet! With a
strangled sound at the back of her throat, she
spun away and left the porch, choosing to go
through the hallway rather than pass close to
where Cam stood beside the outside steps. With
the screen door still swinging behind her, she
took the steps two at a time, and she reached the
bottom just as Cam appeared from around the
other side of the house.

"Look, Kate, regardless of our own problems,
I'd like to think you'd feel free to call on me if
things get out of hand. Dotty was out of line, of
course, but it's not just a case of playing you up
for the fun of seeing the feathers fly. She's
obviously concerned and took the first means at
hand to offer you some sort of protection. I'm
perfectly willing to pretend an engagement to
you if it will give that lout second thoughts about
tackling you again, and I won't even require any
guarantees or release forms signed first." His
tone of voice was above reproach and she could
read nothing behind the bland surface of his
lean, dark face. She had her suspicions, all the
same. Either he was having a quiet laugh at her
expense or he was going to heroic lengths to
relieve his grandmother of any concern. Either
way, she was not having it.

"Look, for your information, I'm almost
twenty-seven, Mr. Greyville," she told him, eyes
blazing in the relentless sunshine, "not seven-
teen! I've been around enough to know how to
handle Tony Palani or any other man who gets
out of line, and the day I need your help will be a
long time coming!"

"You've a short memory, Miss Brown, but

don't worry—you've made your point," he replied in a dangerously soft tone. "With an attitude like yours, you won't spend much time in
fighting off advances anyway." And with that
ambiguous statement he turned and left her
there, as if she no longer mattered at all.

Smug and egotistical creature! He evidently
got a large charge out of making her look a fool
on the beach—probably thought she was an easy
mark just because she had allowed him to kiss
her that night on the wharf, as if she were some
love-starved spinster who'd welcome any attention he might offer her in his spare time! Well,
he'd find out that Kate Brown didn't need his
condescension. She'd make it through the rest of
the summer without any assistance of any sort
from him, and if he got lonesome for his simpering little redheads, then he could just go back up
north again and cool down!

With new starch in her backbone and a no-
nonsense gleam in her gray-green eyes, she
found Tony Palani a cinch to handle. Why had
she ever considered him a threat? The poor dolt
was simply a terribly young, terribly spoiled kid
with too much money to be sure of his worth as a
person, and if he had to keep trying out his
charms on the opposite sex, it was only to assure
himself that he amounted to something in his
own right. His good-looking face had greeted her
with an anxious smile when she stalked into
Gray Lady, and within half an hour they had laid
out the ground rules for his visit.

He would stay until Friday afternoon, paint
with her on location as an equal, and they'd go
Dutch on expenses. There'd be no foolishness or
he'd find himself flat on his back in a bed of

sandspurs, she told him in a voice that brooked
no argument, and the young man took it without
so much as a snicker, despite the fact that she
was a good six inches shorter than he and at
least thirty pounds lighter.

In a way, she regretted her lost privacy, but,
on the other hand, it was nice having someone to
keep her on the go, to prevent her from flopping
down on a bed of dried eelgrass and moping over
an oaf who had passed a few idle moments
trying out his macho skills on her just because
she happened to be the only available female
under fifty at the time.

The next morning she met Dotty on the bridge.
Kate was on her way to the post office and the
walk had appealed to her as a means of working
off some of the restless nervous energy that had
kept her awake far into the night. The older
woman smiled tentatively, then said, "Morning,
Kate. I do hope you've forgiven me for meddling
into your affairs yesterday." The two ripe-olive
eyes in their bed of wrinkles peered out ruefully
and Kate thawed immediately.

"Oh, I know you meant it for the best, Dotty.
You must have noticed, though, that your grandson and I don't exactly hit it off. Both too bossy
and set in our ways, I guess."

"Mmmm, well, yes, I suppose it could be that.
I'll give the matter some thought and see if I can
come up with a solution," Dotty Greyville offered, resting her basket on the railing of the
humpbacked bridge.

"Don't bother. I'm sure neither of us is losing
any sleep over the matter. Cameron . . . Mr.

Greyville certainly has too much to do to waste any time tending to my business."

"Oh, well. He has spent a lot of time surf fishing lately—not that I've seen much in the way of results. He goes out nights, says he can't abide competing for space during the days, but it'll soon be too late in the season for that, and then I don't know what he'll do. Can't seem to settle down to his work like he used to. Shame that pretty redhead of yours . . . What was her name—Sheila?" Kate supplied the name and Dotty continued, "It's a pity she had to leave, just when they were getting to be such friends."

"Yes, isn't it?" Kate allowed through stiff lips.

"Oh, well. He's gone now. Something came up at the plant and he took off before daylight. No telling how long he'll be gone this time." With a vinegary twist of crimson lips, she added, "I only hope he doesn't bring that noisy little secretary of his back with him. After keeping my hearing this long, I'd hate to lose it to something called 'Boogie on Down!' "

Kate's energy sagged and she reminded herself, apropos of nothing, to start taking her vitamins again. "Is that likely? I don't mean about your hearing, but I've enjoyed the respite, too."

Shrugging thin shoulders under a cerise gauze top, Dotty allowed as how it was all too possible. "She actually works for the second in command, but she hops on down here after Cam at the least excuse since she's his when he's in New York. He gets a kick out of her—says he admires her open avarice a darned sight more than any mealy-mouthed hypocrisy. That Bar-

bara, for instance—she was Ivor's wife. Thank
the Lord she's not a Mrs. Greyville any longer. I
absolutely hated sharing my name with the likes
of her!" She waved a hand impatiently and said
she hoped the greenheads weren't starting up.

Barbara, Bebe—Kate could see why a man in
Cameron's position would be wary. He was too
damned attractive for his own good, and to add
to that there was the enormous wealth—some of
it inherited, but most of it earned, according to
his doting grandmother. "But Dotty," she said
suddenly, remembering something, "his car is
still in the garage."

"Oh, he had someone pick him up and take
him to Billy Mitchell Airport. He keeps the
smaller plane here for quick trips."

Bloody swank! Kate bid her friend good morning and continued on her way up to the post
office, anxious to get a letter off to Iola urging
care in the handling of France's impatience.
Kate was doing everything in her power to
collect enough for her sister's London trip, but if
France was going to get into a state and quit her
job to lie about for the rest of the summer, then
something would have to be done.

The next few days passed quickly, with Tony
on his best behavior, and if they seemed flat, it
had to be because Kate was waiting for the next
group of students to come in on Sunday. Her
painting had improved and she told herself, only
half jokingly, that it was because she had herself as a teacher this past month. It was odd, in a
way, that sometimes she had listened to herself
explaining a particular point and thought, Good
Lord, I didn't know I knew all that. It was as if

once she relaxed the grip on her conscious mind, she was able to dredge up everything she had learned during years of studying and observing, things long forgotten intellectually.

Tony was not bad at all, either, and on his last day, while they were packing up their painting gear before going out in search of a seafood platter, he mentioned Stella Wright. "I could have gone for her, you know, if she hadn't got her sights set first on Greyville Electronics. She's bone lazy, but damn, when you look like that, who needs to be useful?"

"What did she know about Greyville Electronics?" Kate teased, rolling her sable brushes in bamboo placemats for safekeeping. "Did it ever occur to you that some women might consider Cameron an attractive man? I'd never heard of the company until Dotty told me what he did for a living."

At that Tony let out a hoot. "Fat chance, doll-face! Dad's store sells a line of his pocket calculators and mini-TVs, but most of his things are industrial. Does a lot of export contracts, I think. Besides, anyone who reads the financial pages knows about Greyville, and believe me, a delectable predator with an eye to the main chance wouldn't miss out on a bet like that if he looked like the dog's dinner!"

Not that Cameron had seemed to mind, for all his disdain of mercenary females, Kate thought with a tightening in the chest area. When one looked like Stella, or even the more obvious Bebe, no man was immune. Which only confirmed what she had said in the beginning: Men—who *needed* them! She had her painting,

and from the looks of things, she was just now
beginning a career that could grow into something particularly satisfying over the years. She
might even try to place some of her better things
in a gallery while she was in the area.

The new group came in on Sunday and
Cameron returned on Monday morning, while
Kate was busily lining them up on the other side
of the bridge. In spite of Dotty's insistence that
Cameron wouldn't mind their spreading out a
bit now that he knew they were a harmless
bunch, she held to her original orders. The rusty
cab she had seen around the village bounced
over the bridge and Cam got out in front of Bay
Oaks, and Kate, who was studying him from
behind the screen of her dark glasses even as
she taped down a sheet of watercolor paper, saw
him reach up and rub a hand across the back of
his neck while he handed over some bills to the
driver.

He looked tired even from this distance, and
different somehow, but then she had never
seen him in a business suit before. After removing his jacket to reveal a lean torso that
tapered down to flat hips, he loosened his collar
and tugged impatiently at the tie before turning
in her direction and waving the driver off.

As he came closer, Kate began to sketch
frantically, mindlessly, ruining a perfectly good
piece of 140-pound d'Arches, and that, in turn,
made her unreasonably angry with the man who
had paused on the bridge to survey the ragged
row of students scattered along the waterfront.
Sunlight glinted on the gold tips of dark hair on

his arms where the sleeves of a light blue shirt were folded back, and the hair on his well-shaped head looked as if he had been plowing his fingers through it. There were new lines across his brow and slashing down his lean cheeks and Kate felt a sudden, overwhelming urge to pull that leonine head down on her breast and stroke away the signs of weariness.

"Sun gets pretty rough out here, doesn't it?" he asked, strolling off the bridge and coming to a halt behind her. "The grove of trees over there beside the house looks as if it would be a better bet. At least it might prevent a few cases of snow blindness."

There was a terrific glare from the white paper—all the same, Kate looked at him suspiciously before relenting. He *did* look tired, and if he were trying to make amends for his earlier hard line, then who was she to refuse? "I suppose you're right," she admitted grudgingly. "I'll consider it later on in the week if we get oversaturated with this view."

"Big of you," he retorted shortly, turning away to cross the bridge without another word.

Oh bother, what on earth made her act like an ungrateful wretch when he had taken the trouble, as tired as he was, to walk across the bridge and make a generous offer?

By the second day, the group had settled down to a good working pace, with the usual division of abilities—a few delightful surprises, a few hopeless cases, and the bulk competent amateurs. Kate loosened up the tight ones and tightened up those who needed a bit more

control. Back at the house, she discussed the
lack of a housekeeper, listened to their offers of
help, and resigned herself to doing most of the
chores, as usual. She found that when people
paid the price she was asking for two weeks'
tuition they weren't particularly eager to spend
much time cooking or doing dishes once the
novelty had worn off.

On a morning when the thermometer threatened to blow its top and there was not a breeze
to be found anywhere, she gave in and herded
her charges to the other side of Bay Oaks, to
the shady grove of trees. Unrepentantly, she
claimed the bench as her own and dropped down
with a sigh while the others set up their stools or
easels or spread their plastic and beach towels
on the ground, according to their own particular
working preference, and then she pointed out to
them from where she sat the various aspects of
the view to be taken into consideration.

They were trudging back for lunch when Cam
called to her from the house. He was standing in
the doorway, and when she climbed the six
shallow shell-and-concrete steps to the porch,
the hallway behind him looked cool and dim and
infinitely inviting.

"Call came for you half an hour ago," he told
her.

"Why didn't you call me? I wasn't that far
away," she snapped. The heat was making her
short-tempered.

Cameron took a long, infuriating draught of
something that clinked with ice before answering her. "I took the message and promised to
pass it on. There didn't seem to be all that great
a hurry."

"Suppose you let me decide that, if you don't mind!"

"Out of sorts, aren't we?" he murmured maddeningly, looking cool and unfairly handsome behind the screen door.

Kate felt the trickle of perspiration down her back and she felt grubby and mean and unattractive and ridiculously close to tears.

"Don't you want to know what the message is?"

"Oh! Well, tell me then!"

He opened the door and she found herself drawn into the inviting coolness of the hallway, prickles, bad temper, and all, and she glared at him expectantly.

"Woman by the name of Iola—your mother, I believe—said to tell you that France had tossed her job and that they were taking off to join you and spend the rest of the summer at the beach with you. You're to expect them sometime after dark."

If there hadn't been a wall behind her she would have fallen. "Tonight? Are you sure? They couldn't! I told her . . . " She broke off in dismay.

"Bad news? You don't want them then? A little too late for that, I'm afraid, but really, Kate, your mother sounded like a delightful person to me. Still, you're the best judge of that, I guess." He finished off his drink and, as if it had just occurred to him, asked if she'd like something cool and refreshing. "You look as if you could use it," he finished, not making matters any better.

"Thanks," she muttered absently, her mind on other things for the moment, "but I've got to fix lunch for my group." Still, she could not seem to find the strength to pull herself away from the coolness of the pecky cypress paneling.

"Let them fend for themselves for once. You can't wet-nurse a bunch of fully grown adults twenty-four hours a day and be effective as a teacher. Come on. Dotty's got a shrimp salad and I'll open you a beer to go with it."

Like a spineless jellyfish, she allowed herself to be washed along with the tide, and when he pointed her in the direction of the bathroom with a terse order to wash up, she obeyed with unnatural meekness. She splashed cold water on her face, her neck, and her arms, and her royal blue sleeveless top as well. Iola and France here! Tonight! What on earth was she to do with them? Where could she possibly put them? France, as usual, simply did as she pleased with no attempt to justify or rationalize, and Iola, who should know better, went along with her. Not a grain of common sense between the two of them, Kate bemoaned silently.

Eileen Greer, the daily, whom Kate had seen several times in the grocery store at Hatteras, smiled at her when she emerged from the bathroom and directed her to the porch, where Cameron and Dotty waited. As soon as she reached the door, she felt a heavenly breeze that seemed to have sprung up from nowhere and she felt suddenly a bit more capable of facing up to her latest problem.

· The table was already set for three and she complimented the Greyvilles silently for their skilled hospitality. No awkwardness when an unexpected third showed up.

"I feel guilty," she admitted, putting aside her

injured dignity to accept the chair Cameron offered. "They're over there at Gray Lady making do with cold cuts while I'm here being served a feast."

"Gray Lady?" Cameron's thick brows lifted crookedly.

"Oh, it's just a silly name I gave the house when I first got here. It looked so much like a woman I know—I used to think of her as the gray lady because she always wore it, and her hair—well, you know how it is. Sometimes, things make you think of people."

She accepted a serving of the delicious-looking shrimp salad and slices of melon, and for a while they contented themselves with doing justice to Eileen's talents in the kitchen. Dotty managed to put away an amazing amount, considering her size and the fact that she interrupted every other bite to remark on something or other.

"And now," Kate said finally, pushing her chair away from the glass-topped table, "if I may use your phone, I'd better see if I can line up some accommodations for my improvident family. It won't have occurred to either of them that I'm not exactly in a position to welcome them at the moment."

"I wouldn't think of it, Katie," Dotty exclaimed.

Kate had already started to rise and now she hesitated, taken slightly aback. "Well, of course, there's a pay station at the . . ."

Cameron took her wrist and urged her back into her seat. "What my grandmother means, Kate, is that we'd be delighted to have them stay here. There's plenty of room and it would provide her with company when I have to hole up in my study for hours on end."

"Oh, but that's out of the question," Kate protested, but she was no match for the Greyvilles. She had no idea why either one of them should go out of their way to accommodate her, but then she was not in a position to refuse outright. She knew for a fact that with the tourist season in full swing rooms were scarce and both Iola and France made no bones about the fact that they preferred first-class accommodations.

"At least allow me to reimburse you for their keep," she pleaded. "I would have done as much at a motel. Oh, and that reminds me, Mr. Greyville . . ." she added, when he exploded.

"What happened to bring on all this formality, for heaven's sake? I think we've gotten well past that stage, don't you, Kate?" He gave her a meaningful look—one that was not lost on his grandmother—and asked her what she had been about to say.

"I owe you some money." Tony had wasted no time in handing over the check she had mailed him, saying he had not even thought of paying for a space he wasn't occupying in her class and that, while he hated to spoil his image, he really couldn't take credit. Which left only one possibility.

"What, something not covered in your lease?" Cameron teased now. "Broken a window or something?"

"Not at all," she replied firmly, determined to set matters straight now that they were on terms of relative peace. "After Tony left the first time, I found some money on the kitchen table and I took it for granted that he left it to pay for the class he had planned to take and . . . well, didn't. You see, he knew that I had a no-refund-after-a-certain-date policy, and . . . well, of course, under the circumstances I couldn't take his money, so I mailed him a check." She felt the hated warmth creeping up her throat and she plowed on relentlessly. "It just didn't occur to me that . . . I mean, just because you . . . well, I'll pay you back." She finished desperately. Good Lord, you'd think she had left any savoir faire she possessed on the other side of the Coranoke bridge! It had certainly been in short supply ever since she got here—at least where Cameron Greyville was concerned!

"Keep it. Apply it to your rent," Cameron said curtly.

"But I can't do that," Kate protested indignantly. "It's not my money, it's yours."

He shrugged. "Okay, so return it. I'll give you a receipt for it to make it all nice and official. Will that suit your tidy little idea of what's appropriate?"

The coolness was back on his face and Dotty broke in with a hasty change of subject. "Let's see now—your mother might like the front room, only that gets the morning sun, and your sister—how old did you say she was? Twenty? We can put her in the room Bebe uses. There are twin beds in there anyway, in case worse comes to worst." She cut her grandson a piquant look and he got to his feet, the black scowl on his face not inviting further comment.

"Oh, dear," Dotty said, watching his expressive back disappear through the door into the

house. "He gets so touchy at times. I wonder if
it's Bebe? Maybe I shouldn't be so outspoken
about her. After all, she is a pretty little thing,
and she does keep the others off his back. You'd
be amazed at how many women try to ingra-
tiate themselves with my grandson. But then
again, maybe you wouldn't," she finished with a
wicked smile on her aged face.

Chapter Five

Kate managed to make it through the rest of the session by dint of filling every hour as full of activity as possible. If she had allowed herself time to think, she might have sat down and wept.

Her family, true to form, had arrived in style. France had blown her severance pay, plus the last of Iola's quarterly check, on a trade-in. The old Ford might not have made the trip, granted, but to trade it in on something so outrageously impractical as the disreputable yellow Spitfire was the height of insanity. Her mother—that dreamy, impractical divorcée who at the age of forty-nine wore floating chiffon to do her lick-and-a-promise housework and used an injured knee shamelessly when the occasion arose to get all sorts of preferential treatment—

the very idea of her traveling across the state in an open sports car with a stagestruck all-but-teenager! Neither of them had a brain or a penny between them, and it had been more than Kate could take to see the pair of them settled into Bay Oaks with the ease of old family friends.

It didn't come as a surprise that Dotty and Iola hit it off at once, for they were a lot alike in many ways—both complete originals—but to see France hanging on to Cameron's every word as if she had just discovered the source of all wisdom was a bit much. Of course, he, like the big, egotistical oaf he was, fell for it hook, line, and sinker. Few males could resist France's voluptuous little figure, contrasting, as it did, with a cute ingenue appeal of blond curls and melting chocolate eyes, but even Kate, who was used to her sister's winning ways, found it hard to hold her tongue when France, clad in a brown crocheted bikini, wandered aimlessly through the scattered class and utterly destroyed the concentration of every male in the group for the rest of the day.

"I'm going to run into the village to get some milk," Kate said abruptly on the Saturday evening when her class had left. She had dined at Bay Oaks at Dotty's insistence and found herself largely ignored while the two women talked eagerly of common interests and France made a positive nuisance of herself by hanging on to every word Cameron said, asking silly questions that even a blind five-year-old could have seen through. He, of course, ate it up with a spoon, even going so far as to beam fatuously at Kate now and then as if to say, Isn't she precious?

"Hmmm? What's that, dear?" Iola murmured, coming back to the real world for a moment.

"Nothing, Mother, I just mentioned going to the store. I'll see you tomorrow, all right?"

"If you're going into the village, I'll run you in," Cameron remarked easily, laying aside his newspaper and completely ignoring the look of petulant disappointment on France's face. He had been attempting to interpret the stock market news to her, to Kate's disgust.

"I need some cigarettes," he said now.

"Why don't we go, Cam? We could take my car with the top down and Kate wouldn't have to bother," France pleaded prettily.

"Read that article on the money market while I'm gone, pet, and then you'll understand what I was getting at, hmmm? Ready, Kate?"

They were outside before Kate could come up with an excuse not to accompany him and he steered her over to the gunmetal Mercedes. When she stumbled over a root in the shade of a big pittosporum at the corner of the garage, he caught her arm, and she jerked away as if his touch were poisonous.

"My, touchy, aren't we?" he jeered softly, opening the door on the passenger side and closing it after her. She tucked her apple-green skirt closely around her as if the thin cotton might offer some protection from him.

When he climbed under the wheel, he didn't close the door immediately. Instead he turned to face her, and in the dim interior light he studied her face intently.

"Aren't you afraid of drawing mosquitoes?" she snapped.

"You're more afraid of the light than you are the darkness? I wonder why?" he persisted, still in that dangerously soft tone of voice. He closed the door with a solid, decisive sound and then she felt his hands close over her shoulders. Before she could do more than utter an outraged protest, his mouth closed over her own and he hauled her across the console so that she fell awkwardly against his unyielding body. Calling on every bit of reserve strength she had, she remained absolutely still while his kiss threatened to rip the very soul out of her, and when he pulled his mouth away to curse softly, "Kiss me, damn you," she felt a tiny thrill of defiance. But then, when his fingertips brushed over her sensitized skin to linger on the racing pulse at the base of her throat before dropping to her breasts, she crumpled without a whimper, and when she felt the inflaming touch of his thumbs as they brushed the aroused nubs of her nipples, she groaned and opened her mouth to the plundering depredations of his tongue. Overwhelmed at her own response, she suddenly pushed against his chest, shaking her head frantically in rejection of her own frightening desires.

"What's the matter?" he murmured against her trembling mouth. "Don't you like what we can do to each other?"

She struggled away from him, bruising herself on the gearshift, and slapped frantically at the door latch, hearing the metallic click even as the darkness shimmered with his low, sensual laugh.

"Leave me alone!" she demanded turbulently. "Let me go!"

"Quit acting like an outraged virgin, Kate," he provoked, his hand finding her breast in the darkness with unerring accuracy. He cupped the throbbing roundness with one determined hand while with the other he forced her to face him once more.

"Why didn't you bring my sister if this was all you were thinking about? She's obviously besotted with you for some unknown reason and she might have welcomed your disgusting advances!"

"Now, is that any way for a woman your age to look after her younger sister's welfare? Katie Minerva Brown!" he mocked, using her hated middle name. "And here I thought your family's well-being was your dearest concern. Have you been misleading me all this time?"

The hand was playing with irresistible effect on her aching breast and his warm breath played on her overheated face and Kate could hear the sound of her own blood as it rushed like a tidal wave through her veins. "D-don't make fun of me, Cameron. I'm not in your league and we b-both know it," she whispered desperately.

"And what is my league?"

"Stop it!" The words were torn from her and she heard the tears in her own voice even before she felt the cool wetness on her cheeks. She sat rigidly in the darkness, her arms clenched at her sides while the man beside her played on her traitorous body like a virtuoso, and she was totally unable to stop him even when her nerves screamed at her that she was in greater danger than she had ever been in in her life before. The fact that the danger was only half understood made it all the more frightening and she shut her mind to the stunning pleasure his skilled, persuasive touch was bringing her.

"Katie, Katie, why can't you relax and just let nature take its course? You want me and we both know it, so why pretend?" His mouth came closer and he insinuated the soft little words against her stiff lips with a touch as light as a whispered promise. Then, with his mouth still hovering a breath away from hers, he taunted, "Why not, Katie? Why not?"

Because I love you, you fool, she screamed silently, and it would kill me to be another in your lineup of momentary distractions!

"I hate you, Cameron Greyville," she heard herself saying in a voice she hardly recognized as her own. "I hate you for making me feel this way! I hate you, do you hear me?" she whispered hoarsely in a choked sound that tore through the brittle tension, shattering it into a million meaningless pieces.

"No you don't, Kate," he replied tiredly, moving away from her. "But you've left it too long now, I'm afraid. You'll never be more than half a woman, and soon that half will grow so embittered that you won't even be able to smile at a man without cracking your shell." He started the engine while she sat there, paralyzed, at his side. "And to think I believed you were only waiting for some poor fool to awaken you. There aren't any Prince Charmings anymore, Kate. It's an extinct species, I'm afraid. So go on back to sleep in your castle and let the briars grow up around it."

Before she could get her breathing under control, they were at the store.

"Do you want to go inside, or shall I get your milk?" he asked in clipped, impersonal tones.

"Please," she replied huskily. "Will you? A gallon, please."

He slammed the door and she sat there in the neon-fractured darkness, watching the summer people through the plate glass with huge, unseeing eyes.

Cameron dropped her off at her own place, and before she was even through the door he had spun away with an angry roar, throwing up a fine spray of sand to sting her legs. She let herself in with leaden motions, and by the time she was ready for bed, her mind was safely encapsulated within the narrow confines she allowed it, going over the checklist and ticking off items against the arrival of tomorrow's class.

A week passed during which she saw practically nothing of her family. Cameron left the island each night soon after dark. Sometimes he was alone and sometimes he had France with him, and once he had all three of the women in his household with him. Kate watched them disappear over the bridge with a bitter longing in her eyes before she turned to the woman beside her and began explaining how to paint convincing reflections.

She continued to use the shady grove on the other side of the Greyville house. If Cameron wanted to rescind permission, then he would have to tell her himself. She had spoken to him only once since that disastrous night and that was when he brought over a letter to her that

had been put in his own box at the post office by
mistake. He was as impersonal as if she were a
transient renter on his property, here for a few
short weeks and then gone without a trace.

Which was nothing less than the truth.

On the next to the last day of the session, she
sent her group on to the house for lunch and
wandered down to the beach beyond the shady
grove, swinging herself down to the hard-packed
sand and walking thoughtfully along the water's
edge. She sidestepped mounds of glistening wet
eelgrass and carefully averted her eyes from the
pile where she had dozed not too long ago,
fighting off a feeling of desolation that threatened to engulf her.

On impulse, she turned and began to wade out
into the shallow water. She wore old sneakers
with white shorts and T-shirt and the warm
water crept over her ankles, her calves, and up
to her knees with a faintly unpleasant tickling
sensation. She stepped over clumps of oysters
and sidestepped murky patches of grass, jumping when a large hard crab scuttled out from
beneath her foot.

The channel was quite a distance off, judging
by the color of the water, and since she wasn't
consciously trying for any particular goal, she
stopped when she felt a current of cold water
strike her legs. It occurred to her that she'd
enjoy a trip to the ocean side and a brisk,
refreshing dip in the Atlantic. As long as she had
been here, she had yet to swim in the ocean,
although she and Tony had stopped at one of the
drive-outs and walked over to see if any of the
surf fishermen were having any luck, and once

she had stopped alone, watching a group of surfers waiting patiently out beyond the bar for something large enough to get them ashore again. But it hadn't occurred to her to take off an afternoon and go swimming. There had been no one to go with her and she didn't relish going alone.

You may as well begin to relish doing things alone, my good girl, she pointed out to herself, because that's the way you're likely to be doing most things from now on. She was wading slowly back toward the shore, her eyes focused on the refracted brilliance of the surface as she tried to avoid submerged hazards. Not until she was in ankle deep water did she dare to look up again, and when she did she halted, her heart leaping painfully before settling down to an increased rate of speed.

"I wondered if you were trying to wade all the way to Englehard," Cam remarked. He was standing at the edge of the water, the sun gleaming on sweat-dampened shoulders, and she found herself quite unable to lift her eyes to his face. His legs were braced apart—long, tightly muscled limbs whose tan was modified by the coat of crisp, dark hairs—and his hands were planted on his hips above the low-riding white shorts he wore. There was something so overwhelmingly masculine about him that Kate was embarrassed at her own reaction. As a result, when she came within ten feet of him and stopped to speak, her words sounded sharper than she intended.

"What do you want?" she asked ungraciously.

He held out a hand. *"Pax,"* he said, and she was compelled to wade closer until she touched her reluctant palm to his. "I've brought an invitation to lunch. When we didn't see you go back to Gray Lady with your charges, it occurred to me that you might be needing a break. You're going at it too hard and heavy, Kate. Why don't you readjust your schedule so that you'll have more time to yourself?"

She bristled, but when she would have withdrawn her hand, he gripped it more tightly, and she looked up at him helplessly. "I can't shortchange my students, Cameron. They're paying for so many hours a day and they'll get it."

"But do you have to throw yourself into it quite so wholeheartedly? You're out before any of the others . . ."

"I have to plan the lesson," she interposed.

"And you're the last one tagging in . . ."

"Someone has to pick up the bits and pieces they leave behind."

"And then you're back out there before you've even had time to put away a decent lunch—which you also make for them. You're shortchanging them as it is, Kate. Nobody can put out and put out indefinitely without either breaking or having the quality compromised."

"What would you know about teaching art?" she demanded fiercely, and this time she succeeded in pulling her hand away, folding it unconsciously in her other hand as if to protect something inside it.

"Nothing, but, Kate, what I've said goes for any enterprise that utilizes any degree at all of creative energy. You're driving yourself and you're getting as gaunt as a scarecrow. Not even that lovely tan you're developing can cover up the shadows under your eyes. You look haunted,

Katie." His voice took on a tender note that threatened to undermine her, and she lifted her head instinctively, bracing herself against the powerful spell he could weave so easily. "Give yourself a break during the heat of the day, at least. If you delay your afternoon class until after four, you can rest during the hottest part of the day, have a late lunch and a late dinner."

"And what about my evening sessions?" she demanded with some asperity. "Shall I begin those at the witching hour?"

"It might be fitting."

She caught the gleam in his eye and couldn't help but answer it with a rueful smile. "All right, you've made your point; I'm deteriorating badly. So I'll consider it, but only because it just occurred to me that I have yet to go swimming and at least once while I'm here I want to lower myself under a cold wave and stay there until the sun goes down."

"I'll take you one day next week, if you like. Now, how about lunch with your family and Dotty, and before you refuse"—he grinned, holding up a staying hand—"I'll be busy in my study so it will be strictly a hen party. I'm afraid your mother thinks you've been neglecting her lately."

They had come to the bank by now and she reached automatically for the overhanging branch to pull herself up, and when his hand covered hers on the rough bark, she turned to him, her gray-green eyes bright with apprehension.

"Don't look at me that way, Kate. I'm your friend, whether or not you want to think so."

"You could have fooled me a couple of times

there," she told him crisply, pulling her hand out from under his.

He didn't try to stop her but swung up without benefit of the branch, and his long legs strode along beside her shorter ones, easily matching her agitated pace. "I plead guilty to a nasty disposition, but only under conditions of extreme provocation."

"Exception noted but disallowed," she quipped, unable to remain distant with him in this disarming mood.

They reached the house and went on through the hall and Cameron told her to wash up if she wanted to and then she'd find the others out on the side porch. "I'll get on with my work, if you don't mind. It's not always easy to find the time in *this* household."

She gave him a stricken look and he caught her hand. "Forget it, Kate. I didn't mean that. There are other pressures that you know nothing at all about." The look he gave her was indecipherable and she let it go. It was too hot to fight today, and besides, she found it altogether too easy to succumb to Cameron Greyville when he was being charming.

And even when he was not, she concluded wryly.

"Where's Cam?" France greeted her when she joined the others.

"He mentioned some work. Hello, Iola. Is that a new dress?" She dropped down into a chair with a warm smile for her hostess and Eileen served her a cold plate and a glass of iced tea.

"Do you like it? I've never worn this color before and I rather fancied it. What do you think, Katie? Tell me honestly."

I give up, Kate cried silently, sampling a bite of scallops vinaigrette with dill. The faster I accumulate a nest egg, the more they throw away.

"I suppose you're still mad about the car," France pouted.

"Frances, it's not that, honey . . ." she began.

"It's *France!* Please, Kate, it looks like you *could* remember that, but all you think about is your silly old students! You never even consider Iola or me. Anyway, when I start the Academy I'm going to be France Capella. What do you think? I mean, Brown just doesn't have it. I'll have to use Mother's maiden name instead."

"All right, France Capella then. But, honey, how can you expect to start anywhere when as fast as I collect any money you spend it? It costs more than you think just to hold body and soul together here in the States, but once you get to England, it's going to be rough. It's not as if you could hop over there, audition, then come home again to wait for the results. You'll have to stay until the whole thing's done, one way or the other."

"But you're getting it together, aren't you? You said this class of yours would . . ."

"Look, France, I'm sure Dotty is bored by our private affairs, so we'll discuss it some other time. Iola, have you seen the museum yet?"

Ignoring the hint to keep family matters private, Iola knocked the wind from Kate's sails by telling her that the apartment was taken for the rest of the season. "You see, Mrs. Anderson's daughter and her husband wanted to come while Mrs. Anderson had her operation and it worked out just fine. They'll stay in our apartment and pay the utilities, which will be a big savings for us. So that's all to the credit side, and then there's the article I did on astrological gardening. I'm sure to get something for that," she finished eagerly, her nearsighted brown eyes, so like her youngest daughter's, glowing with a childlike pride.

"Iola, the almanacs have been writing articles about astrological gardening for hundreds of years. What do you know about either subject, for that matter?"

"Well, I can read, can't I?" came the irrefutable reply.

"Kate, try some of this cheesecake. You need fattening up," Dotty offered, cutting off a king-sized portion.

"No thanks, Dotty. It's really too hot to eat, isn't it? Iola, just how long were you and France planning to visit?" Kate asked firmly.

"Oh, what a rude thing to ask!" France exclaimed. "We only just got here, and besides, Cam's promised to take me surf fishing some night."

Oh, I'll just bet he has, Kate thought grimly. A bird in the hand, after all. She pushed her plate away, refusing more iced tea, saying she had to return to her classes, and then France broke in with a bright suggestion.

"Katie, I know of a woman back home who gets enormous sums for private lessons. Not classes, you understand, but one-on-one stuff. Why don't you scout around Hatteras and see if you can't pick up a few private students?"

"And when would you suggest I fit them in? Between dinner and breakfast? The light's not all that good then, you know!" Kate snapped.

She was close to tears and she could think of no real reason. After all, neither her mother or her sister had changed at all. France had the beauty, Iola had the lovable personality, and Kate had the business head. They couldn't all have the same positive qualities, but there were times when she thought some were more positive than others.

She had reached the door and turned back to thank Dotty for the delicious lunch when she heard a chair scrape in the room whose windows opened out onto the porch, and with a sinking feeling she knew that Cameron had heard every word they had said.

The wretch! He had deliberately hidden himself away in there to eavesdrop on her—as if he didn't know more about her than any mortal had a right to know about another person's business anyway! And now he had heard her berating her mother and her only sister, and he'd be thinking her even more hard-bitten and selfish than he already did!

Chapter Six

On Saturday morning, after one group left and before the arrival of the next, Cameron sent word by Dotty that he was going surf fishing and wanted to take Kate along. "You'll love it," the older woman declared. "I went with him once on one of his nighttime expeditions and it's another world, watching the phosphorus glowing on the waves and sparkling in the wet sand, and the gulls. They sound different when you can't see them—like something out of *Paradise Lost*. I kept letting him throw my line out and hoping I wouldn't catch anything and my luck held."

What the devil—why not? The summer was already half over and there were so many things she hadn't done. Unfortunately, she *had* done the one thing she shouldn't, and the very fact that she had been so foolish as to fall in love with a man who considered her some sort of joke

118

was enough to insure that she look elsewhere for her next workshop location. Maybe Ocracoke next year, or further north, at Kitty Hawk or Nags Head, but not Coranoke—not if she had to run the risk of getting involved all over again. It was going to take more than one long, hard winter to get herself over this disaster, as it was.

But while she was here, she may as well try it all. So, according to Cam's instructions, she wore her shorts and took along a jacket, and when she climbed into the front seat, she found a very disgruntled France glowering at her from the back.

"What are Iola and Dotty doing tonight?" she asked, more to break the uncomfortable silence than out of any real curiosity.

"Going to a meeting of some sort, I believe," Cam told her when France remained silent. Trust Iola to get herself involved in local activities on a summer visit.

They parked at the end of a gravel road and trudged over the high, soft dune, each of them carrying something. France still had done no more than grumble a short answer to a direct question but Kate was determined not to let her spoil the outing. They topped the dunes and she felt the soft, damp wind strike her face. It held tantalizing hints of exotic shores thousands of miles away. On a more mundane level, it was sufficiently strong to keep the mosquitoes at bay, and for that she was grateful, although she was not terribly bothered by the pests anyway. The moon was three-quarters full and it played tag with dark, silver-edged clouds, illuminating the writhing glow of the breakers in a beautiful, mysterious way.

"It's absolutely magic," Kate said, turning impulsively to where Cam was rigging tackle onto three rods in sand spikes.

"Holding a rod and reel gives you an excuse to spend as much time as you like enjoying it without feeling like a damned fool," he returned, and she could hear the smile in his voice.

"Well, I can think of better things to do, but under the circumstances . . ." France let her voice trail off peevishly and Kate was in no doubt as to the circumstance she meant. She had no intention of letting her sulky little sister spoil things for her, however. France had things all her own way most of the time, but tonight Kate was going to enjoy herself. Tomorrow it was business as usual, but for a few hours she could forget the effort of juggling eight artists without wounding any tender sensibilities.

"Done any fishing before?" Cameron asked her as he baited her double rig with shrimp.

"Not much—lake fishing, mostly, and that was ages ago."

While he tended to France, throwing out her line for her when she squealed that she couldn't see how to do it in the dark, Kate edged as close to the creaming breakers as she dared and let fly. She backlashed, cursed softly, and backed up, untangling as she went, and when Cam called over and asked if she were all right, she told him blithely that she was fine, little knowing what her bravado was to cost her before the night was out.

She cheated and reeled in the line over the worst tangle, then waded out and cast again. It might not go far, but since she couldn't see, what difference did it make? Like Dotty, she didn't really care whether or not she caught anything; it was enough just to be here, watching the moonlight on the water, the tiny blinking lanterns of fishermen further down the beach, and knowing Cam was standing nearby.

The fact that France was on his other side, demanding most of his attention, did little to dispel the magic of the moment, for Kate was nothing if not a realist. Men would always prefer someone like her adorable little sister, and who could blame them? But that didn't mean that Kate might never know the satisfaction of times like this—times when she could pretend that the tenuous friendship might end in something more. What was the harm in dreaming as long as you *knew* it was only a dream?

"I'm going back to the car! You two can stay here drowning shrimp as long as you want to, but my skin's tender, and something out here is about to eat me up!" France declared loudly.

"I haven't felt a thing—have you, Kate?" Cam asked, taking France's rod and planting it in the sand spike before returning to take up his position at the edge of the water.

"Not a thing. Guess I'm not very sensitive to them," she replied, pushing away an uncharitable feeling of glee. After all, it was no laughing matter to be itching from insect bites, and France *did* have a lighter complexion.

"We'll be back before long. Nothing seems to be biting tonight—at least underwater. Play the radio or tape, if you'd like. The battery can take it." Cam tossed her the keys and returned his attention to fishing.

After a while, a snatch of music drifted over to

the surf and Kate hummed along with a half-forgotten song about never loving again. Cam appeared at her side, reeling in to check his bait.

"Bored?" he asked.

"Nope. I don't think I've ever been bored in my life, and certainly not tonight. This is something special, isn't it?"

"I thought you'd like it. Thank heaven Dotty isn't depending on us to bring home the bacon, but then she's used to my luck as a fisherman. The only thing I ever catch are skates, shark, and the occasional stubborn hard crab."

"I've heard that you can eat sh— Cam!" she screamed. "Something's happening!"

"Well, hang on, don't panic. I checked your drag and it's fine. Reel him in."

"But, Cam, he's reeling *me* in! Take it—you do it!" she cried, trying to hand off her rod to Cam, but he backed away, putting his own rod into a sand spike in order to coach her along.

"All right. Lean back, then take up the slack. Let him go a little if you have to, but be ready to . . . whoa, don't horse him, you'll lose him."

He coached her, soothed her, and gentled her along, and she fought against the monstrous strength at the end of her line, but it was a losing battle. She was getting deeper and deeper into the surf, the water breaking about her hips, and Cam was right behind her, encouraging her to bring him in, not to get out too far.

"You've got plenty of line, Kate, so let him run. Let him wear himself out if you have to—just don't give him any slack!"

"But that's just it," she wailed. "I had a backlash and I reeled in over it and . . . Oh, no!" The moon went behind a thick cloud, plunging

them into darkness just as Cam told her to lean
back and begin to take up, and she leaned.

What happened then was never quite clear.
There was a loud snap and her foot slid down an
embankment, and the next thing she knew, she
was being pummeled and rolled by thundering
tons of water. The absolute horror of feeling
herself at the very bottom of such an overwhelming force and being dragged relentlessly
out to sea lasted only moments, but those moments extended inward on her consciousness as
if they were an eternity. It only occurred to her
much later that her life had not flashed before
her eyes; the only thing she could think of was
Cam. Somewhere out there in the night was
Cam and she would never see him again.

And then she was being pulled apart, her arm
grasped and held against the strength of the
Atlantic, and she felt herself being dragged back
up onto the hard-packed sand, flung down on her
face, and pounded. Or at least it felt that way.
She never quite lost consciousness, but she was
beyond speech, beyond telling Cam that her ribs
were fragile and that she had been scraped over
every inch of her body, so that when he turned
her and began to breathe into her mouth, she
was more aware of gravel digging into her skin
than she was of his mouth on hers.

The next few hours were a kaleidoscopic
nightmare. She had insisted on walking into the
house on her own two feet so as not to alarm Iola
and Dotty, but when France reported the Spitfire
still out, Cameron scooped Kate up in his arms
and took the steps as if she weighed no more
than a child. She began protesting halfway up
and was still at it when he shouldered open a

door and laid her on top of an elegant brown spread on a king-sized bed.

"I'll ruin it! I'm all wet and sandy. And you should have left me at my own place. Cam, please, won't you . . ."

"Please, won't you shut up? Kindly allow me to know what's best for you, Kate Brown. Frances, go and fetch your sister something to put on!"

"Which room is hers?" France had yet to spend more than five minutes at Gray Lady and those were spent during the last open house exhibit. Now Cam muttered an inelegant phrase and ordered her to look after things until he got back.

"Are you really hurt bad, Katie?" France asked anxiously after the sound of the slamming door signaled Cam's departure.

"Of course not, silly," Kate croaked, surprised at her growing hoarseness. "I just got the wind knocked out of me and swallowed gallons of sand and salt water. Just let me lie here for a few minutes and then I'll go on home. Look, France—don't tell Iola, all right? She'd just dither and there's nothing to worry about now. In fact, the only casualty was Cam's rod and reel. Lucky for me, he grabbed me first, and by then the darn fish had probably taken the rod all the way to Diamond Shoals!"

"Oh, don't worry, Cam can afford it. Besides, he said your fish broke the line, so maybe the rod and reel will wash up in the surf someday."

"I wouldn't hang around and wait." Kate coughed and asked for a tissue. "Lord, I feel awful! I must look terrible!"

"You do," France told her frankly. She

touched Kate's hair and then wrinkled her nose in distaste, brushing her hand on the seat of her shorts. "Well, if there's nothing else I can do for you, I'd like to get a bath and put lotion on my bites. Honestly, Kate, they almost ate me up!"

"Well, you ought to know better than to wear so much perfume. It attracts them," Kate pointed out, wishing her sister would leave. There was nothing very restful about her company and Kate was growing more miserable by the second.

"Maybe I'll get used to them after a while. They say if you stay down here long enough you don't even notice them," France said, strolling over to the mirror and examining her face for blemishes.

"Just how long are you planning to stay?" Kate implored.

"Honestly, you just can't stand it, can you?" France swung around, hands on her hips and her dark eyes flashing. "You weren't fool enough to think you had a chance with Cam, were you? The only man who ever looked at you twice was that stodgy old Hal Brookwood, so why should you care if Cam and I . . . well, *he* wants me here! If you don't like it, then why don't *you* go somewhere else? I'm Cam's guest and you're just his tenant, so if anybody leaves, it won't be me!"

With an exasperated sound, Kate sat up and swung her feet to the floor. Her head rocked and she lifted a hand to her forehead, but dropped it when she saw France's dubious look, making a deliberate effort to hold on to her temper. "Look, France, this is obviously a man's room—Cam's, I guess—and if he put me in here, it means that the other rooms are all filled up, and it's just not fair for you and Iola to move in on somebody you don't even know and stay the whole summer long. Don't you realize that they might have other friends who'd like to drop in for a week or so? There's no room!" She had to stop and try to clear her throat and the effort was agonizing. Swallowing all that salt water was hard enough, but coughing it back up again had been brutal! "So don't tell me you'll stay just because he hasn't asked you to leave—he won't do that and you know it. But how do you suppose I feel, knowing that if I hadn't been here in the first place then he'd have his house to himself?"

France shrugged her beautifully formed shoulders. "Look, it's too late to cry over spilled milk now. Cam and I *did* meet and, what's more, we like each other—like each other a good deal, as a matter of fact—so you really don't have anything to do with it anymore. We have an—an understanding, Cam and I. He'll do whatever I want him to do, and if you're nice to me, then I might . . . I just *might* get you a rent reduction." She smiled and the movement of glossy pink lips was in no way reflected in her innocent-looking eyes.

Kate was across the floor in less time than it took to consider the action. She spun the younger girl around by the shoulders and shook her, although her own strength was not up to more than a token effort. "Now you listen to me, Frances Brown. If you dare do anything stupid and get yourself in trouble, you'll have me to answer to, not Iola! You've caused her enough grief in the past, and this time—I'm warning you—you behave yourself or you'll have me to deal with and I don't deal lightly!"

"Stop it, you hateful old thing!"

France's cry came just as the bedroom door opened to admit Cam, and as soon as he appeared, a light green nightgown draped over one arm and a glass of amber liquid in his hand, France let out a wail and launched herself at him, tears flowing like a summer rain down her becomingly flushed cheeks. "Cam, make her stop it. She's been perfectly dreadful to me, and I just can't take anymore!" She buried her face in his chest, causing the drink to slosh alarmingly, and when the other arm came automatically around her, he lifted an eyebrow at Kate, who stood wavering on her feet, her eyes wide, clouded pools of distress.

"What's been going on here?" he asked mildly, resisting the younger girl's efforts to pull his ear down to her mouth as she whispered soft, frantic words at him.

"She says she doesn't want us here! She says I have to go and take Iola with me, and she's just saying that because she's jealous!" The tears in no way hurt France's looks, and as she tipped her face up to see what effect her words were having on the man who held her, Kate felt worse than ever; unlovely, unloved, and unwanted, as well as desperately sorry for herself—a rare feeling and one she deplored.

Cam was murmuring comforting, soothing words to the distraught girl in his arms, and she shuddered deliciously and blinked through tear-bejeweled lashes. "She's always been jealous of my beauty, Cam—ever since I was a little girl and everybody always told Mama how darling I was—and now she wants to get rid of me and I don't want to go. Please say you won't send me away, back to that hateful old job where I melt to death because they're too cheap to use the air conditioner."

A bubble of mirth arose in Kate's throat and she dropped down onto the bed again as laughter overcame her. Her head was splitting and her throat was raw, but it was so funny, so absolutely, melodramatically bad theatre, that she howled. And then the laughter changed imperceptibly to something else, and her face crumpled, and she sat there with her hands hanging limply at her sides and cried openly— big, agonizing gulps that shook her slender frame, not lovely, helpless tears like those her sister was pouring out all over Cam's shirtfront.

There was a flurry of movement seen dimly through shimmering eyes and then she was lifted up and moved over, cradled against a warm, hard wall that rocked with the rhythm of a heartbeat. "Hush, Katie," Cam murmured, rocking her as if she were a baby. "Hush now, it's not important."

The sobs slowed and finally ceased, and she sniffed, hiccoughed, and hiccoughed again. "Oh, Lordy, once I start these, it takes forever to get rid of them," she wailed in her painful, raspy whisper.

"Well, you've already had your scare, so I'll have to try my own favorite remedy on you."

"What's that?" she sniffed weakly, looking up at him through a blurring tangle of wet lashes. He was leaning against the headboard and holding her against him, her sandy, wet hair

spread out over his shoulder. She knew the
answer to her question as soon as the words
were out and she did nothing to avoid him. His
mouth closed over her own and she hiccoughed
once and then her arms wound around his neck
and she gave herself up to the powerful medi-
cine of his lovemaking. Gone, too, were all
thoughts of France and the hurt of watching the
amused tolerance with which he treated her, the
affectionate indulgence he had shown toward
her from the first. There was only the knowledge
that his mouth was devouring her and his arms
were imprisoning her. And when she felt his
hands at her buttons, she could only shrug and
help him ease the uncomfortable garment from
her shoulders. Her shorts came next, and he
eased them from her hips and down over her
legs without ever breaking contact with her
throat, where he was branding her with a down-
ward trail of kisses.

"It'll probably take a fish scaler to get all the
gravel off your skin," he murmured, scratching
lightly against her midriff to loosen the tiny
grains that seemed to be embedded there. He
held her breast in his hand and picked the small
shells off deliberately and Kate turned away
from his overpowering nearness.

"You shouldn't be here," she protested weakly.
"You shouldn't see me this way." Her skin was
stinging, her bones were aching, and her throat
was raw, and overcoming all that was a delicious fever that started somewhere in the pit of
her stomach and spread to all her extremities,
leaving her weak and defenseless.

"Your inhibitions are showing, Katie darling,"
Cameron whispered, trailing the backs of his

fingers down her thigh, making her acutely aware of the fact that she wore only a pair of wet nylon pants and a lacy bra that did little to cover her.

He lowered his face to her throat again, finding all the most sensitive places, places that telegraphed frantic messages to the rest of her body.

Between tiny, nibbling kisses, Cameron teased her, telling her that her hair looked like seaweed, that there were few openings for mermaids this season, but even though his words were light, his tone teasing, she could sense the rapidly increasing tension in his own body and his eyes—those tawny pools of amber—were strangely dark and intense under heavy lids. He made no attempt to hide the state of his arousal, and when he spoke, even though his words were light, they were torn between deep gasping breaths and shaken with the pounding of his heart. He licked her throat.

"Hmmm, salty—sandy, too," he whispered, "but delicious." His hands moved again and she was released from the constraint of her bra and it felt so free, so fine, when his lips moved to the gentle hills of her breasts and conquered them, teasing the straining tips with his tongue.

"Ahhh, Cam, please," she groaned, hardly knowing what she was pleading for. The waves of shuddering pleasure that overcame her drove all thoughts of the recent past from her mind, and when she felt the weight of his body moving over her, she accommodated herself to him with an abandon born of instinctive knowledge and he trembled, his own desire no longer in control.

"Kate, darling—I must have you." He uttered

the words in a voice that was hardly recognizable as he fumbled with his own clothing.

Borne along too far, too fast on the tidal wave of passion, Kate heard nothing until she felt Cam stiffen and draw away slightly from her burning flesh, and then she heard the door slam and Dotty's voice as she called out to see where everyone was.

With a half-stifled cry of pure frustration, he lifted himself from her, allowing the coldness that struck her dampened skin to creep into her heart, and when she cried out a hoarse protest, he reached out to touch her face with a trembling hand. "God, Kate, I'm sorry. I had no intention of allowing things to get out of hand. I'm sorry."

Her very nerves screaming, she forced herself to reply flippantly, "Oh, that's all right. At least my hiccoughs are cured. Now, if you don't mind, I'd like to put on my c-clothes and g-get out of here!"

All her senses unnaturally alert now, she could hear France's voice and Dotty's and Iola's shocked interruptions and she knew it would be only moments before the invasion. "Please," she entreated.

"Kate—let me help you into the bath. You need to wash that sand and salt off you and I'll change the sheets—you can't sleep in a sandpile." He half-lifted her from the bed and she jerked her arms away from him.

"You've helped me quite enough as it is, if you don't mind! What did you do with my shorts?" She pulled the corner of the bedspread over her as a protective shawl, for all she wore now were her damp nylon panties. "And stop staring at me like that! It's not the first time I've been kissed, believe it or not! You can just chalk it up to another n-near miss!"

"Stop trying to be so tough, Kate. We'll continue with this another time."

"Oh no we won't! You can parade all the cute little popsies you want through your bed, Cameron Greyville, but not this girl! If there's one thing I'm forewarned about, it's lecherous, amoral, tomcatting men, and I refuse to be a part of it!"

Her voice was rising and she couldn't seem to help it, and he raised a hand and slapped her. She hadn't taken her eyes from him for a single moment while she released all her bitter, frustrated words, and she saw, even as his blow rocked her, the tiny hesitation, as if his muscles refused to obey his command, and she saw him flinch as if the blow had landed on his own cheek, and then he hauled her to him and cursed softly into the wet tangle of her hair.

When Iola called nervously through the door, he told her to come on in, and even then he didn't release her. "She's shocked and she took a pounding, but basically she's all right," he told the anxious woman who had paused uncertainly just inside the door to stare at the sight of her oldest daughter, clad only in her underwear, held fast in a man's arms.

Kate still had a part of the bedspread caught up around her bare shoulders, the rest of it trailing across the bed, and she sniffed and said, "It's all right, Mama. I just got in over my head, that's all." In more ways than one, she added silently.

She pulled away from Cam, raking him with

an accusing look as she snatched up her night-gown from where he had dropped it. The forgotten glass of brandy was still on the bedside table and she picked it up and tossed it back in one gulp, choking as it struck her raw throat. The tears streamed from her eyes again, and as soon as she could find her voice, she said, "Will you two please get out of here? I'm perfectly all right and I can take care of myself without any help from anybody!"

Iola darted away, never one to argue with her strong-minded daughter, but Cam stood his ground for a minute more. "You'll get into that tub and soak yourself thoroughly, and if there's any more of this foolishness from you, I'll come in there and scrub you down myself!" He followed Iola from the room, banging the door behind him, leaving Kate standing there more utterly confused than she had ever been in her life before.

Chapter Seven

In spite of a strong compulsion to return to Gray
Lady and her own stark little bedroom, Kate was
glad to fall into Cam's king-sized bed after
soaking away part of her aches and pains. She
awakened the next morning after an almost
stuporlike sleep to find herself stiff and head-
achy, but infinitely better than she had been
before. She examined herself and found that the
only visible signs of her ordeal, aside from
pink-rimmed eyes, were a bruised cheek and a
knee and elbow that must have skidded for
miles on a gravelly ocean floor. Not too bad,
considering the alternatives. Her throat still felt
sore, but that was improving by the minute as
she began to stir.

When awareness of her emotional ordeal
began to surface above her physical complaints,

she did her best to ignore it, but there was no forgetting, no avoiding the knowledge that Cam had come very close to seducing her last night—with her full cooperation, unfortunately. Now, to her utter shame, she regretted the interruption. Just a few more minutes and she would have known what it was like to be made love to in the fullest sense by a man who had come to mean more to her than any living creature.

It was lust, not love, she reminded herself, but all the same, she wished . . .

Snap out of it, you silly old fool! she whispered fiercely to herself. He saved your neck once last night, but it was Dotty and Iola who saved it the second time. That would have been a fine state of affairs—you in bed with the man who, for all you know, might end up your brother-in-law!

Dotty came up with a dress for her to put on and reported no sign of any students so far, and, after dressing, Kate descended the stairs with a slow, awkward gait, well aware that besides the unusual pallor of her face, her cheekbone bore a bruise that gave her a slightly raffish look. She was determined to hurry over to her own house before she had to face anyone else. Dotty's bright, curious sympathy had been bad enough without having to run the gamut of the others.

Cameron emerged from his study just as she reached the bottom step and his tawny eyes missed nothing of her appearance. "All better now?" he asked, his searching look seeming to signify more than just her physical well-being—or maybe she was just being overly sensitive. There was no reason why he should even give it a second thought, that petting session that had ended so abortively. It was certainly nothing important in his life, and as far as she was concerned, it was nothing to her either.

"Fine and dandy," she replied brightly. "I might scare off a few of the more sensitive students today, but maybe if I tried a new hairstyle, a Veronica Lake look, it would cover the worst of the damage." She reached up and pulled a swathe of dark hair over her injured cheek. "What do you think? Do you fancy this? No? I suppose it loses something in translation." She dropped the hair with a glittering, brittle smile and said, "So be it—they'll just have to harden themselves then."

"I told you before to stop trying to be so tough. It doesn't convince anyone and it doesn't become you. If you have a minute, I want to talk to you about canceling out on this session." He reached for her arm and she jerked it away, her eyes wide and accusing.

"You what?"

"You heard me. You're in no condition to teach, Kate, and you insist on driving yourself in weather that's a drain on anybody's energies, without that mess last night. You can call them now and probably reach most of them before they set out, and if you refund the fees, they'll sign on with someone else and everyone will be a lot better off."

"Well, thanks a lot! That's a real vote of confidence if I ever heard one. Let me tell you something, Mr. Greyville—you may be my land-lord, but that's *all* you are! We have a business arrangement—no more, no less—and nowhere in my lease does it say that you can give me orders on how to conduct my business!" She came down the last step and brushed past him, throwing open the door with a force that sent it clattering back against the wall. "Thanks for the use of the bed!" she flung over her shoulder as she stalked off into the blinding, relentless sun.

The students came on schedule, a mixed group as far as ages and abilities were concerned, but Kate didn't doubt her ability to take them and mold them into a working unit. She had done it before and there was no reason why this class should be any different. She did, however, re-schedule her afternoon class to a later hour, and since that made the nightly critique and demonstration session correspondingly late, she changed the format slightly so that it was peer critique, leaving her free to relax while her students discussed one another's work.

She avoided Cam, and after a few days she was chagrined to notice that he was avoiding her as well. He was embarrassed by what had so nearly happened that night he took her fishing, she told herself, not stopping to think that embarrassment hardly equated with what she considered his true character. She saw him from a distance often enough, usually with France, who hung on to him as if she were in dire danger of blowing away.

Well, if Iola, living right there in the same house, didn't care what was going on under her very nose, why should Kate bother herself about it? Let them move in lock, stock, and barrel for a marathon visit. Let France make a fool of herself over a man almost old enough to be her father. Kate was tired of trying to sort out the affairs of a couple of scatterbrained females who didn't seem to need her anyway!

None of which made her sleep any easier. In the airless humidity of midsummer, her room took on aspects of a steam bath, and she sweltered as she stared at the ceiling and tried to force herself to relax enough to drop off to sleep. She had scheduled herself another free week between sessions, if she could only last out, and this time there'd be no Tony Palani to bother with either.

On the last day of classes she took her gang to the grassy stretch alongside the wharf. She might not have Cam's permission to use his boats, but he couldn't object to her painting them, surely. The session was one that required a good deal of demonstration on her part, for several of the students were having trouble understanding the complex curves of a boat well enough to draw them. She gave several analytical diagrams, pointed out a relatively simple method for putting together perspective with proper symmetry, and when time was up, she left them to struggle with their own attempts. The sun beat down on her straw hat, burning her shoulders through the apple-green top and even the tops of her feet above her sneakers.

She had seen Cam's car drive off soon after class began and had not noticed it return, and she thought it might be a good time to drop in and see if Iola and France wanted to go to Manteo and Nags Head with her tomorrow. Dotty, too, if she were interested.

Slinging her gear into the canvas hold-all, she emptied the sand from her shoes and set out, head down, face shaded by the brim of her straw hat. She could hear Dotty's tuneless whistling from the garden and from an open window upstairs came the sound of France's radio. The music was not exactly to her own taste, but it was a darned sight quieter than some she could name.

She rounded the corner, swooping to inhale the fragrance of a window box of nasturtiums and phlox, and straightened to see a tangle of bare legs dangling from the hammock on the porch. After the brilliance of the open sunlight, the porch was shadowy and cool, and she stood there blinking for a few seconds before the legs sorted themselves out into two distinct pairs, one brown and covered in hair and the other tanned, sleek, and decidedly female. From her low angle of view, she could see little, but she gradually became aware that Cam was regarding her with a cool, quizzical look, and she bit her lip in vexation at being caught out again.

Just as quickly, she got herself in hand. It should certainly come as no surprise to find him thus engaged. After all, this was exactly where she had come in. All the same, the feeling of betrayal persisted until she quite forgot why she was there in the first place.

"Were you looking for me, Kate?" Cam asked laconically.

Another head popped up at that and she found herself staring back at Bebe Gonlon's petulant prettiness. Bebe made no pretense at being glad to see her. In fact, of the three of them, only Cam seemed perfectly at ease, but then nothing could shake his careless poise.

"Are you still here?" Bebe demanded rudely.

"Are you back again?" Kate came back, just as rudely.

Cameron threw back his head and let loose a rich chuckle, pushing the red-gold blond away as if she were a kitten he had tired of playing with. "Ladies, ladies, there's room enough in the hammock for both of you. Care to climb aboard, Kate? It seems to have an irresistible appeal for some unknown reason."

"I was looking for Iola. Don't let me interrupt anything," she insisted rancorously, turning on her heel to leave.

"Kate?" The one word, spoken softly, but with underlying firmness that was unmistakable, stopped her in her tracks and she turned back in spite of herself, to see a look on Cam's face that baffled her completely. It was almost as if he had reached some conclusion that satisfied him immensely and had just now had it confirmed.

That afternoon she took her group to the oak grove on the other side of the main house. It was as cool a place as they were likely to find on a day like this. The fact that it was directly overlooked by the side porch at Bay Oaks had almost caused Kate to change her mind, but the weather's demands won out, and now they were getting set to put into practice all they had learned over the two-week period. Kate worked on her own watercolor, a full-sheet impression of the Hatteras shoreline, with a line of boats of all sorts providing a blindingly dramatic contrast against shadowed foliage and deep blue sky and water.

There was little discussion, for everyone was concentrating, and occasionally someone would wander over to look over Kate's shoulder and return to their own work with fresh perspective. The class's compulsive hummer hummed away tonelessly and it blended in with the drone of pollen-laden bees, bothering no one.

And then the peace of the afternoon was shattered by a burst of rock and roll at a decibel level that carried full strength from the porch at Bay Oaks to where the little group of painters stood in momentary shock.

"Blast it all!" Kate cried, throwing down her brush in disgust when a blob of dark green fell into a flawless sky from her startled hand.

The volume was modified, but only slightly. It was still disruptively loud, and she was tempted to march right up on the porch and snatch the radio and throw it as far out into the Pamlico as she could. It was Bebe, of course. There was not all that much difference in her and France's musical tastes, but at least France was more considerate when it came to volume. Living in the apartment, she had had to be.

They discussed the matter for several minutes and Kate collected a few highly original ideas for solving the problem (some not practical within the boundaries of the law), but it was she herself who hit on a logical, easy countermeasure. It took less than five minutes to locate the tape she wanted and then to drive her station wagon into position and open all four doors without being too obvious.

When the first strains of the Wagner aria were heard, full volume, there was pandemonium for about three minutes and Kate didn't think she was going to be able to go through with it. Poor class—they had their hands over their ears but they were laughing uproariously. Poor Wagner, too. He was not Kate's favorite composer, by any means, but he certainly didn't rate being used in a battle with punk rock.

"Uh-oh! Here comes trouble," Margo Lane remarked in a loud whisper.

Bebe Gonlon flung herself down the porch steps, her bottom lip looking as if a bee had stung it, and marched across to where the class was assembled. Hands on her hips, she lit into Kate with a tirade, half of which was lost, under the circumstances, but that didn't stop her. Her eyes were blazing and her voice climbed stridently to end on a shrieking note when the music was suddenly stilled.

Cameron closed the doors of the station wagon gently and strolled over to where the confrontation was taking place. Kate, her blemished watercolor hopelessly dried now, was glaring at Bebe, taking everything the younger woman could give her while she refueled for her own outburst.

Her temper was completely defused when Cam swatted Bebe on the bottom and told her to run along. "You're outgunned, outnumbered, and outclassed, honey, so better pack it in." Then he turned to Kate, the laughter still lurking in his eyes and a suspicious quiver at the edge of his mouth. "Sorry, Kate. It won't happen again. I only wish I'd thought of it myself." He turned and sauntered back to the house, catching up with Bebe halfway there and dropping an arm across her drooping shoulders.

Kate watched them disappear into the house, and it was some time before she realized that her fists were still clenched at her sides. She frowned belligerently at her watercolor, ripped it off the board, and packed away her gear.

Chapter Eight

Having arranged to take France and Iola with her for a day at Manteo and Nags Head to do the galleries and browse the shops, Kate was outside rinsing the salt from her windshield before the sun had even cleared away the morning haze. She heard the front door at Bay Oaks swing to and looked up in time to see Cameron, a bag in each hand, standing on the porch talking to his four women.

Iola saw her and waved and then France, with a hesitant look at Bebe, threw her arms around Cameron's neck and whispered something in his ear—or at least it appeared that way to Kate, where she stood polishing her glass until it squeaked protestingly.

She wadded up the paper towel in her hand and closed her eyes just for a moment. Oh, how it hurt, in spite of all her fine resolutions to act

her age, to resign herself to having no part in
Cam's life, and smile if it killed her when she
had to watch him treating France and even Bebe
with the casual affection she coveted so much.
Not that casual affection was all she wanted
from him, but even that looked good from where
she stood on the outside looking in.

"Ready? Dotty says the shops at Nags Head
and Kitty Hawk are scrumptious! I could use a
new beach robe and maybe a new pair of sandals." Iola settled herself into the back seat and
spread her skirt around her, conscious of the
lovely picture she made, as Kate well knew.

They waited for several minutes before France
joined them, and Kate started the car impatiently as soon as her sister was seated. Neither
of them spoke until they had passed through
Hatteras and were almost at Frisco. Not that it
mattered, for Iola kept up a steady line of
inconsequential chatter from the back seat,
depending on no one for replies. France seemed
to be wrapped up in her own dream world, a
world, Kate saw with a certain pang, that
brought a secret little smile to her lips as she
gazed out at the ocean that played hide-and-seek
with them all the way to Oregon Inlet and
beyond.

Kate dragged them, unwilling, through the
galleries, and they insisted on spending equal
time in the shops. It was too hot to wait in the
car, so Kate went with them, and she bit her
tongue and remained silent while they both
spent far more money than they really ought to
have on what they considered irresistible bar-
gains.

It was when they were on the way home that

Iola mentioned the extension course she had signed up for at the high school and Kate turned to her in dismay, almost running off the road before she recovered her wits. "What on earth did you do a thing like that for, Iola? Those things last at least six weeks, don't they? Good Lord, I'll be leaving myself in a couple of months. I thought you were only here for a short visit." That last was pure sarcasm, for Iola had never spelled out the duration of their stay in spite of Kate's hints. She continued in desperation, "Besides, France will be leaving for England pretty soon and then how on earth will we get both cars back home?" Iola could do short stints behind the wheel but with her bad knee long drives were out of the question.

"Oh, you needn't worry about me, Kate. Cam and I have already made our plans," France said from beside her, still with that secret little smirk on her face.

"What plans?" Kate demanded, feeling a coldness that began in her middle and spread rapidly to her extremities.

"Never you mind, fusspot. We didn't tell you because we thought it might upset you—we know how you are—but Cam understands me better than anyone ever has. He's going to take care of me and then you'll be free to do your own thing. He might even let you have the house if you want to do another of those workshops."

Over my dead body, Kate vowed silently. She was glad she had on her wraparound sunglasses, for France was peering at her with a curious, sidelong stare and Kate had never been too good at concealing her emotions. If her impulsive tongue didn't betray her, her clear gray eyes would, reflecting her every thought with devastating frankness.

She took a deep breath and pulled up behind a line of traffic that was waiting for a house trailer to negotiate a turn. Fine time to move a blasted thing like that, she thought with unfair vehemence, pushing the brake hard against the floorboard to relieve some of her feelings. She said, as they were nearing Coranoke bridge, each word pulled from her with difficulty, "I think you'd better tell me just what your plans are, Frances."

"Sorry," her sister replied blithely, "I promised Cam I wouldn't, but you'll know soon enough."

"But I'm your sister," Kate agonized. From the back seat came a gentle snore and Kate gripped the steering wheel until her hands hurt.

"That's just it. Like I said, Kitty Kate, you'll know soon enough. Just a hint, then. Pretty soon you won't have to wear yourself out trying to keep up with me. I'll have someone else to do the job, so you should be happy. Lord knows, you've complained often enough."

That hurt. Not so much as the idea of France and Cam together, but enough to make her duck her chin into her collar defensively. "I only hope you know what you're doing, France. I don't want you to get hurt and I don't think you've known Cameron long enough to be sure of the sort of man he is. We had an example of . . . well, that's water over the dam," she ended, making up her mind to say no more about what was patently none of her business.

"Oh, don't worry about me. Cam's a marshmallow," her sister said airily.

"I'm surprised you'd allow your marshmallow to spend the day with Bebe Gonlon then. She obviously has a sweet tooth, too," Kate remarked with wry bitterness, swearing silently that that would be her very last word on the subject.

"Oh, he took her to Norfolk to the airport. I'm not worried about Bebe. She's been after him for ages, but he only puts up with her because he feels sorry for her. Her father worked for Greyville and he got in trouble with the law and now he's doing time, so Cam lets Bebe get away with murder because he feels responsible. Well, he's not, of course, but you know Cam," she shrugged. "Anyway, he says she's a good little secretary, but when she gets on his nerves, he just tells her to trot her carcass."

"Frances Ann, I don't know where you pick up slang like that," Iola said sleepily from the back seat. "Kate never talked that way and I know I never did."

They pulled up before Bay Oaks just as the sun sank into the Pamlico Sound, and like a rerun of an old movie, Cam appeared with Hal Brookwood in tow.

"Hi, Katie! I made it—just like I promised," Hal called out, his nice, regular features split into a wide smile. He had obviously showered and dressed after he arrived, because his hair was still damp at the edges and the tan leisure suit was creased in all the right places.

"Hello, Hal," Kate managed to say pleasantly as she helped Iola out of the back seat and started handing out packages. "I didn't see your car in the driveway."

He pointed to a respectable-looking sedan under the shade of the oak grove. "Cam said it would be better off there instead of out in the broiling hot sun. You haven't had dinner, have you? I thought we might go out somewhere."

Feeling like the tag end of a bad day, the last thing Kate wanted was to have to spend an evening playing the part of a congenial companion, but she was Hal's hostess, after all, so she smiled and told him to give her half an hour.

As it turned out, they went out with Cam and France, and that was a hundred times worse. It seemed there was a fish fry at the home of friends of Cam's and the whole matter was settled by the time Kate emerged on the scene again. Without a reasonable excuse, there was nothing she could do but go along with the others. At least she wouldn't have to spend the evening alone with Hal, feeling quilty everytime he focused those nice spaniel eyes on her so hopefully.

She had dressed quickly but with gratifying results. Her navy blue skirt teamed beautifully with a kelly green halter and matching espadrilles and she had attached a pair of outsized green hoops to her ears and allowed her dark hair to swing freely about her shoulders. A slash of crimson lipstick was all the makeup she needed, for her eyes were dramatically light against her becoming tan. The last thing she had reached for before rushing out of the house was a bottle of scent, but after a brief hesitation she had put it down unused, deciding to settle for being merely clean. Leave the enticements to those who wanted to entice.

Their host and hostess were a nice middle-aged couple named Sam and Inga, and Kate

talked to them both briefly about her workshop,
having seen them at one or two of the openings.
They were interested in art in general and
specifically in local scenes with which to deco-
rate their handsome new home.

Kate and Hal followed the tour with half a
dozen other couples as Sam showed off his four
balconies, two overlooking the Sound and two
cantilevered out into the pines and dogwoods for
shade and privacy. On one a large grill was
sending out tantalizing odors as a variety of
seafood was being prepared, and on another, a
few feet away, several people were dancing to
the music of hidden speakers.

In spite of herself, Kate had a delightful time.
Hal found a fellow balloon enthusiast and
France had discovered someone who knew
someone who had won an Oscar, so Kate was
able to relax and pretend an interest in the
marinading of seafood that was being argued
about good-naturedly beside her.

Cam, she noticed, seemed content to relax in
an enormous lounge chair and sip his highball,
contributing nothing to the cheerful hash of
voices, and it was some time before Kate realized that his eyes were following her about as
she wandered from group to group. At first she
had put it down to coincidence, that odd force
that made two people in a crowded room look up
and catch each other's eyes, but when it happened over and over as she strolled around
examining the original art, approving most and
delighted to find no reproductions on the walls,
she grew ill at ease. She came to a framed
mirror and was immediately caught and held by
the reflection it gave back: Cameron, his long

limbs and lean, powerful body concealed, but in no way disguised by the white slacks and shirt he wore, leaning indolently in the doorway, watching her.

There was an opening leading to another level and she hurried through it, aware of his silent movement behind her as he stalked her through the large house. This was ridiculous! She was half tempted to turn and confront him and see what he had to say about such childish behavior.

She didn't feel at all childish, though. Instead, she felt peculiarly vulnerable. The sounds of music and conversation seemed to come from a great distance as she came to the sliding glass panels that opened out onto one of the wooded balconies.

He was right behind her and slid the tinted panel closed, leaning against it to level a quizzical smile at her. "I thought you'd be basking in your lover's warm gaze tonight."

"I seldom bask in public," she said shortly.

"My error. I should have considered that when I insisted you both accompany France and me to the party, but I'm afraid I didn't stop to think."

There was no hint of apology in his voice as he moved away from the door, and Kate backed up until she came to the peeled cedar column. "You never do if it concerns someone else's preferences, do you?"

"Is that the way you see me?" He seemed amused and it stung her into the familiar antagonism, her protective device.

"I don't see you at all, Cameron Greyville. Don't flatter yourself."

He laughed at that, his eyes expressing open

disbelief. "Don't worry, Katie, the party won't last forever. You and your worthy Hal will have all the time you want back at Gray Lady. Does that make your heart beat faster?"

"Don't make fun of me, Cam—nor of Hal either. He may not be the irresistible playboy type, but he's a fine man, and . . . and he'll be a wonderful family man," she finished a little desperately. Cam was moving closer—intimidatingly, suffocatingly closer—and she had already backed up as far as she could go.

"But will he make your heart beat one split second faster, Katie?" he purred, brushing her hair back behind her ears and fingering her green hoops.

"That's none of your business! I'm past the age when I need a moonlight-and-roses type of romance to have a satisfying relationship with a man!" She jerked her head away from him and slipped past him, but he caught her arm, and she was suddenly sitting down on the edge of a cushioned chaise with Cam leaning over her.

"Good Lord, Katie, don't hand me that! You're light-years younger than your sister and probably always will be in some respects. And anyway, what does age have to do with anything? Do you think your mother's given up because she's fifty? Did you know she's only waiting for the widower in the apartment downstairs to come back from Europe before she hightails it back home? Now don't tell me it's because she enjoys a rousing game of checkers before she goes to bed! Hell, it wouldn't surprise me if Dotty jumped the broomstick again. She'd be well worth any man's time and effort at eighty-one!"

"She told me she was seventy-five," said Kate, bemused.

"She lies a lot and so do you, my fine friend." The words were growled softly, so close she could feel the warmth of his breath against her face, and then there was no distance between them at all as he sat down beside her and pulled her against him. His mouth moved sensually, tantalizingly over her own, tasting, probing, nibbling, and his hands urged her into even closer proximity to his hard, virile body. She knew she should have resisted, knew she was courting heartbreak, but he had only to touch her and all her resistance faded like a dream at daybreak.

And he was touching her. Oh, yes, he was touching her, his hands tracing the line of her jaw, following the sensitive tendon of her throat to the place where a frightened pulse beat frantically. The inner surface of her arms somehow became an erogenous zone as his fingers circled tantalizingly over her skin and the sounds of the party faded away, leaving them cantilevered in space, subject to only their own emotions, their rapidly heightened awareness of the needs of two mature people.

Kate was hazily conscious of the fact that, while her experience fell far short of her twenty-one-year-old sister's, her own body was twenty-seven years old and was waking up to make demands of its own, regardless of her readiness for them.

"Put your hands in my shirt," Cameron urged, not waiting for her to obey as he pushed her hands inside the open front of his white cotton shirt. "Touch me! Here . . . and here. Ahhhh," he expelled his breath in a shaken burst. His mouth moved to the center of her low-cut halter, his tongue tracing the edge of her skin along the jade green border until it came to the shadowy cleft between her breasts, and her own hands tightened convulsively in the thick pelt of his body hair before sliding down his sides to grip his lean waist.

Some fast-fading glimmer of sanity made her protest. "Cam . . . we've got to stop this craziness . . . Hal . . ." Her mind reached out for the only two anchors she could think of—Hal and France—but before she could protest further, Cameron raised his lean, dark face to impale her on a gleam of dark, wicked amusement.

"Brookwood wouldn't know what to do with you if he got his hands on you. You'd blow his circuits wide open." He punctuated the observation with another mind-shattering kiss. "When you're wired for one-ten, honey, you don't go fooling around with two-twenty."

The chaise was narrow and not overly long and somehow there was a tangle of limbs, and they were laughing, touching, kissing, and nuzzling to the accompaniment of two pounding hearts, and Kate pushed the last remnant of thought from her mind, consigning both France and Hal to limbo. Oh, Lord, I'm hopelessly lost, even knowing that he's only playing games, that he goes from woman to woman like a bee in a flower garden and I happen to be the only thing in bloom at the moment.

"Stop muttering to yourself and kiss me, Kate," Cam whispered, unfastening the clip that held her halter around her neck. It fell to the front and he helped it away from her breasts and she felt the warm night air on her bare skin just before he covered them with his caressing hands. "Oh, Katie, what you do to me—but you know, don't you? There's very little I can do to hide the way . . ."

Someone called from the hallway just beyond the door and Cam let go a string of soft, gentle oaths, and then he tenderly replaced Kate's halter, after kissing each aching, throbbing breast, and refastened it behind her neck. "One of these days . . ." he threatened under his breath.

The glass door slid open and France stepped out onto the porch. "There you are! We've been looking everywhere for you! What's going on here, or need I ask?" She came over to the chaise where Cam sat, his back to Kate as she lay there, eyes closed momentarily against the shame and embarrassment of facing France.

"Hal was asking if I knew where you were, and knowing Cam I thought I'd better locate you first. The fish is ready and if you two don't get a move on, there won't be any left."

Cam left first, leaving the two women to follow, and France, sounding as if she were the oldest of the two, said, "Really, Kate, you're too old to go sneaking around making out in dark corners. How do you suppose Hal's going to feel when he sees you with your bare face hanging out?"

"Oh, Lord, my lipstick! Where's my bag?" Kate wailed softly, wishing France wouldn't make everything seem so . . . so sordid!

"The powder room's through there. You'll find

everything you need—maybe not in your shade, but at least you won't look as if you'd been . . ."

"Just stop it, will you, France? I'm sorry, honey, but I'm not as blasé about some things as you are, and right now—well, call it middle-aged inhibition, if you want to, but France, I'm sorry—I really am—it's just—well, it's a party, I suppose. I had two glasses of wine on an empty stomach. It doesn't mean a thing, you know."

"Oh, come on, Kitty Kate, it's no big deal. Anyway, it's all in the family, you might say. Soon will be, at any rate." France skipped off with a giggle, leaving Kate staring miserably after her.

The party lasted hours longer, and although Kate was aware of tasting this and that, laughing, and making some sort of reply to any direct questions, her mind was absent. Wherever it was, it was certainly not participating when she smiled her too-bright smile and said her polite thank-you's, and later, in the back seat of Cam's car, with Hal's arm around her shoulders, she was only numbly aware of France in the front seat, chattering on about the boy she had met who knew someone who knew someone who had won an Oscar.

She was intensely aware of Cam's monosyllabic answers, however. His mind as well as hers seemed to be occupied elsewhere at the moment.

She was only dimly aware of Hal's murmurings against her hair and his arms tightening on her shoulder, drawing her closer to him. It was

too hot and she was in no mood for it and when
Cam approached the Coranoke bridge without
even slowing down, jolting her away from Hal's
embrace, all she could think of was that it was a
good thing they hadn't been kissing—she might
have needed new front teeth.

Chapter Nine

Over the next three days, Hal took her places she had first seen with Tony Palani. The heat was bad, the mosquitoes not bad at all, and the humidity a little uncomfortable, but it was a beautiful island, all the same, and there were plenty of places where one could get completely away and walk for miles without seeing another soul.

She avoided these places. The last thing she wanted was to be alone with Hal, for her absent-minded acceptance of his attentions on the night of the party had encouraged him to think there might be hope for his cause, and there was none at all. He slept at Gray Lady and, after the first night, when she had made her position clear, he had made no attempt to bother her there, saving his melting looks and tentative touching for times when they were on neutral ground. He was a perfect gentleman and all she could feel toward him was a casual interest that varied from lukewarm affection to mild irritation.

Cam offered them the use of the runabout on Hal's last day, pleading the pressure of business as an excuse not to accompany them, and they spent a day on the water, getting as far as Hatteras Inlet, where they watched the shoulder-to-shoulder surf fishermen jockeying for position on shore and the sometimes hair-raising antics of the various boats that circled the inlet in pursuit of fun and fish.

When he left the next day, Kate could hardly conceal her relief, and she had a pretty good idea that she had seen the last of him, except for the chance encounter. He had looked at her accusingly and then his reproach had changed into resignation after she allowed him to kiss her goodbye. "I was afraid of this," he told her ruefully. "I've known you a long time, and familiarity breeds contempt, they say. As soon as I saw the way you look at Greyville, I figured it was no go—even though your kid sister beat you out there. Can't help where the old heart lodges, can we? At least you'll know what I've been going through."

He drove off with a wave of the hand and Kate watched him dutifully out of sight before turning back to the house. There was still the laundry to do and the larder to restock and then another group of students would be descending on her. Four more sessions, with a week in the middle, plus the two weeks she had allowed herself at the end of the term to unwind. She wouldn't be taking that vacation here—that much was certain.

Knowing it would be better if she kept moving, going through the motions whether she felt like it or not, Kate stripped the cots and gathered the rest of the laundry. She stuck a sketchpad and pencil in her purse, for there was always a wait at the launderette and she enjoyed doing quick character sketches. Unfortunately, it engaged only her hand and her eye, leaving her mind free to roam in areas best left alone, but it couldn't be helped. She'd never have the concentration to settle down with a book.

On her way out to the station wagon with her giant load, Dotty hailed her, and she put the bag in her car and walked across to meet the older woman.

"Hi, Kate. Don't you have the nerve to try that old washer you've got? It's ugly as homemade sin, but Eileen tells me it still works. She used it this spring when our pump broke down."

"I can't face the thought of being stuck with a hundred pounds of wet laundry," Kate laughed. "And anyway, I rather like the washday break. Believe it or not, there's something soothing about all that sloshing and churning and I always love the clean smell."

"How on earth did a child your age get so peculiar?" Dotty grimaced. "Well, if you change your mind, Cam will be glad to string up a line out behind the house. The old lines were out where the backyard used to be where the Sound is now. Erosion, you know."

"Thanks, Dotty, but this is fine. I don't need any clotheslines."

"He worries about you, you know—watches you bustling around here when you ought to be stretched out in the shade somewhere, where all God's creatures are meant to spend the summer. But that's not what I wanted to tell you. I've decided to go home with your mother for a visit! What do you think of that?"

Kate was horrified, though she tried not to show it. The trip in the tiny Spitfire would be bad enough—not that she dared mention it to Dotty—but the apartment!

"Dotty, I'm sure Mother would love to have you, but you know we live in a tiny apartment. One bedroom and a sofabed and not much else. It's not at all what you're used to, you know."

"Kate Brown! I thought better of you! Do you think I care about things like that? Your mother and I get along like a house afire! She's a remarkable person and it doesn't matter a darned bit to me if she lives in a caboose on a railroad track!"

Kate was duly chastised. She covered her eyes with her hands and peeped out. "I'm sorry, Dotty, truly. I didn't mean it that way at all. It's just that—well, it gets hot as blazes and our old air conditioner doesn't always work and I just don't want you to be uncomfortable. And it's about four hundred miles, too, don't forget. An all-day drive."

"Oh, that's nothing. Cam will fly us there whenever we decide to go," his grandmother dismissed airily.

"And rent you a car when you get there, too, no

doubt. Had you thought about that?" Kate asked more astringently than she should have. "The Spitfire will be here and Iola won't have any way to get the two of you about."

"Don't you worry one bit about us. As a matter of fact, I think the Spitfire was a mistake, although I like its looks. Iola really ought to have a closed car with her tendency to earaches."

With a helpless look, Kate admitted that she didn't even know about Iola's tendency to ear-ache and dismissed the unworthy suspicion that it was merely a ploy now that her knee no longer drew sympathetic queries. Lord, those three! They were too much for her to keep up with! As a matter of fact, she might as well make it those four, for from the looks of things Cam, France, Dotty, and Iola would be a going concern from now on, needing little, if anything, from her. She might as well make her own plans for the future, now that she was free to pull up stakes and move about as the spirit took her. France and Iola would have Cam to look after them, just as France had told her, so it seeméd as if coming here to Coranoke had been a heaven-sent bless-ing after all.

Try and convince yourself of that, you fine, fancy fool, she whispered to herself as she bumped over the wooden bridge and headed for the launderette.

The next morning she decided to explore Ocracoke, the next island south of Hatteras. She invited France to go with her, but the younger girl said something about having her hair done for a party, so Kate shrugged and turned away. She simply had to get used to the fact that from now on she was odd man out around here. France would have plans with Cam that would certainly take precedence over any tame outings with her own sister.

The ferry ride was exhilarating, especially since she had had the forethought to bring along a bag of stale bread for the gulls. She tossed the crusts, losing herself for a while in the enchantment of soaring, gliding wings against a sky of an intense shade of blue and bottle green water laced with a fine foam of white that blew across the sides of the ferry in a rainbowed spray.

If there were more than a few interested masculine glances at the tall, tanned brunette in white shorts and a yellow knit top, the subject was not aware of them. She threw half her crumbs to the gulls and then gave the rest of them to a small boy who was tearing off bits of paper to try and tempt the graceful beggars.

Ocracoke was a charming town built around a silvered, bowl-like harbor that was accented by clusters of boats. Kate drove around, then parked and walked, following the narrow, sandy roads bordered with picket fences that enclosed thickets of yaupon and oak, yucca and oleander. The day passed pleasantly enough, and if only a small portion of her attention was focused on what she saw and did, then not one of the many tourists she passed seemed to know the difference.

Maybe I should be wearing a Vacancy sign, she thought with a flash of her usual sense of humor, after a woman with three children under five asked her for the second time if she knew where a rest room was. Feeling in need of a quick wash, herself, she decided to drive back up the beach and use the facilities at the ferry landing.

She got within a quarter of a mile of her goal, having stopped to watch a herd of Ocracoke's famous Banker ponies for almost an hour, when she felt a lurch and heard the ominous flop-flop sound that signaled a flat tire. There was nowhere to pull over, for the shoulders were deep, soft sand, and she watched helplessly as car after car sped past on its way to the ferry.

Well, darn! Fifteen minutes later, she sat in her car, all windows open to admit any possible draft, and faced the unpalatable truth. It was almost dark, there was no traffic at all now, and she had no idea how late the ferries ran because she had not bothered to read the schedule. And her spare was flat. She had forgotten to have it repaired after the flat she had had on the way to Coranoke at the beginning of the summer and now she was fresh out of luck!

Not that it would hurt her to spend a night in her station wagon, but she felt terribly alone here on the north end of the highway miles from anywhere. She couldn't even see the lights of Ocracoke from where she was and further along was only a deserted washroom and an empty ferry ship. She hadn't even had the foresight to bring along a flashlight!

For perhaps twenty minutes she sat there staring numbly at the hazy horizon while one by one the stars twinkled out and were reflected below in the lights along the ferry slip and out in the channel. Then, as one winking white light seemed to grow into several and they were bracketed by a red and a green, it gradually dawned on her that another ferry was approaching and that, while her car was stuck on Ocracoke, she was free to cross the inlet. Surely she could get a ride into Hatteras as far as the Coranoke bridge, and then tomorrow France could go with her to buy a tire and retrieve her own car.

Even in the warmth of the July night she felt chilled, and she crossed her arms over her breasts as she jogged along the pavement, still soft from the day's sun. She was almost at the slip when the ferry eased into position, lowered its ramp, and began to disgorge its passengers. As cars crawled off the ramp and picked up speed on their way south, she stepped well off the highway, and when one of them screeched to a stop just past her and began to back up again, she wondered what sort of fool had such a suicide complex.

The remaining two cars from the ferry pulled out and passed and then the car stopped beside her and Cam got out to demand just what the hell she thought she was doing, hiking along the highway alone in the middle of the night.

By the time he had driven with her back to her car to check on the size of her tires, pick up her spare, and set out the emergency flares he always carried, Kate was shivering in earnest, and it was not just a matter of temperature. Cam had spoken no more than half a dozen words to her and those didn't bear repeating, and for the life of her she couldn't see why he was so angry. It wasn't as if it were her fault. Anyone could have a flat, and she hadn't wrecked her car or anything serious, for Pete's sake!

Not until they were crossing the inlet on the way home after having secured a promise from a service station that the tire would be replaced and the car delivered to Coranoke before ten the following morning did he speak to her again, and then she'd just as soon he hadn't. She argued that she was planning to take care of things herself as soon as she got back home and he told her that, at the rate she was going, not a station on the island would be open when she got there, which was why he had called ahead.

"You always have to try to tend to my business," she accused, squeezing herself as far away from him as she could in the close confines of his car.

He ignored her gibe. "Have you any idea what's been running through my mind since you failed to show up at a reasonable hour?"

"As a matter of fact, I haven't." She tried for lightness and failed miserably, due mostly to the uncontrollable tremor in her voice.

"If you ever go off like that again without letting me know where and when to expect you back, I'll have your hide!" he informed her in a blistering tone.

"Now, just a darned minute there, buster! Where I go and what I do have absolutely nothing to do with you, and you'd better get it through your thick head that just because you've got something going with my sister, and my mother seems to have latched onto you like a barnacle, there's no way you're going to start telling *me* what to do! No *way!* I was looking after myself, and France and Iola too, long before I ever heard of you and your blasted island, and when I get to the point that I need someone to tell me when to sneeze and when to say *gesundheit*, I'll look for someone a darned sight more reliable than you!"

He was silent so long she could almost hear her teeth chatter. Her nerves were stretched to the breaking point, and she wished he'd speak, say *something*, even if she had to slap him down again.

"Are you quite finished?" His voice was dangerously mild.

Uncertainly, she nodded. "I just wanted you to understand that I don't need you. I don't need anyone."

"You didn't need anyone to mend that flat you forgot to take care of all summer. You didn't need anyone to remind you to take along a flashlight in your car for emergencies, so you wouldn't break your stubborn little neck stumbling along the highway in the dark!"

"I could have called someone, and it wasn't dark—not completely—and anyway . . ."

"Shut up!" He reached for her and jerked her across the seat and she knew what was coming and steeled herself against it, against giving in to him, when by all rights she should never speak to him again.

But then where Cameron Greyville was concerned her good sense flew out the window when he so much as laid a finger on her—and now it was more than a finger he was laying on her—oh, far, far more!

It was a punishing kiss, a kiss of anger and frustration, and Kate's mouth felt bruised even as she sought more of whatever it was he was offering her. When her hands went from his chest, where they had been entrapped by his sudden move, to slide around his neck and entangle themselves in his thick, alive hair, he groaned and lifted his mouth for just an instant. "This time, woman, there's no escape for you— not until I'm good and ready," he promised her, and when his mouth covered hers again, it was a seduction—a piercing, bittersweet invasion that was an act of possession in itself.

With a surge of desperate strength, Kate twisted her head aside. "Cameron, stop it! Don't do this to me. It . . . it isn't fair," she wailed softly, her hands even then playing traitorously over his hard, rounded shoulders. "You talk to me as if I were an idiot, and then you treat me as if . . . as if I were . . ." She broke off with a gasp as his hands slipped up to weigh the ripe full- ness of her aching breasts, his thumbs stroking the engorged nipples through the covering of her shirt and thin tricot bra. She despised herself for letting him use her in this casual, devastating way when she meant no more to him than any other female he happened to find himself with. He was a potent male animal whose virility could not resist a challenge, and she, Lord help her, was no challenge at all, did he only know it!

Her yellow knit top was no barrier to his discovering hands and when she felt his hard, smooth palm on the cool satin of her thigh, she stretched herself out invitingly, and it could have been the center of downtown Tokyo instead of a dark ferry in the middle of Hatteras Inlet, for all she cared. The delicious shuddering quicksilver that rippled through her body left her devastated, limp, and helpless against his inflamed passion.

There was a sudden lurch and they both

became aware of the changed tenor of the engines as the ferry swung around to engage the ramp and Cam put her away from him with unsteady hands. "Even here there's no privacy. Never enough time," he said with a sigh, bracing himself with both hands on the steering wheel as he stared ahead at the small flurry of activity.

Kate fought back a desire to cry, to strike out at someone and to laugh hysterically as she struggled to put her armor back in place. Huh! Some armor! It remained impervious just long enough to gain her trust, then fell apart at the first touch of an enemy hand.

The engine roared into life and they rolled off the ferry and headed for Hatteras and Coranoke. With trembling fingers, Kate combed through her hair and straightened her clothes and wondered if she looked as totally devastated as she felt. She cast an oblique glance at the grim profile beside her and was irritated to see that he looked as cool and remote as ever—not at all as if only moments ago he had been staking a claim to her body with his conquering hands while his heart thundered in that magnificent chest as if it were about to burst its confines.

"Will you be needing a car before ten?" he asked tersely.

"Not that I know of," she replied just as shortly.

"If anything comes up, you're free to use the Spitfire."

"Oh, are you taking charge of France's possessions now as well as her life?" she flung at him.

He didn't dignify her gibe with an answer and Kate felt thoroughly ashamed of herself. He had

that right, if anyone did. After all, they'd soon be
endowing each other with all their worldly
possessions. She muttered an apology under her
breath and he dismissed it with a brief nod of his
head, and she reminded herself that she had no
right to jeopardize France's future happiness.
Taking on Iola for an in-law was difficult enough
without the addition of a harridan for a sister-in-
law!

"I'm taking you straight home because your
mother has been worried about you," he told
her.

"That I doubt!"

"You never give up, do you? A real tough case.
Whether you know it or not, girl, both your
mother and your sister care a great deal for you,
and when you run off this way and worry them, I
can only think you're totally indifferent to their
feelings." He had pulled up in front of Bay Oaks
and Kate was determined she was not going
inside with him. With first one thing, then
another, coming at her, she was beginning to
feel like a punching bag, and the last thing she
needed now was to have to face France again
after making a fool of herself with Cam. Not to
mention one of Iola's infrequent bursts of mater-
nal solicitude. She'd fall apart if she had to go
through all that right now, and as for Cam,
better his anger than that he even began to
suspect what he'd done to her heart!

She said very quietly, "I think, if you don't
mind, I'll just go on home. I've had a pretty full
day and I'd like to get an early start tomorrow.
It's my last day of freedom, you know. So tell
Iola that . . ."

"That's another thing! Why do you call her by

her given name? Are you so afraid of showing affection for anyone? Would it be a sign of weakness to allow yourself to acknowledge the relationship? *Damn*, Kate!" He opened his door with a snort of disgust and she did not wait for him to come around and help her out. By the time he caught up with her, she was almost at her own front door.

He held her by her upper arms and she just hung there, staring up helplessly at him, glad of the darkness that hid her swimming eyes from his dissecting gaze. She thought he was going to kiss her again and she swayed slightly toward him, unable to prevent herself from responding to his nearness, but he only shook her and released her, telling her harshly to go to bed.

Chapter Ten

If Iola had been worried about her the day before, there was certainly no sign of it when she and Dotty stopped by Gray Lady on their way to the library the next morning. Dotty wore a white hat topped with yellow flowers that matched the jaunty little Spitfire and Kate had to smile at the incongruous picture the two women made— the fifty-year-old with her faded yellow hair in a pony tail and the pixielike eighty-one-year-old with her sun hat and orange-framed sunglasses.

"We're having a wingding tomorrow night, Kate. Eight-thirty and wear something special! It's a celebration!" Dotty called out.

"A celebration of what?" Kate asked with amusement, envying the pair their obvious high spirits.

They glanced at each other like two small children with a secret, and Iola said, "Well, that's not our business to tell, Katie, but you'll know soon enough now."

As if she didn't already know deep in her heavy heart, she thought as she watched the colorful pair cross the Coranoke bridge.

Well, may as well go down with all flags flying. She headed for her bedroom, stumbled over a small stool, which she kicked ruthlessly out of the way, and stood frowning at her skimpy collection of dresses. She had not brought along anything that could be construed as special. There was always the navy skirt and green halter, but memories of the last time she wore that outfit rushed in on her and she turned away.

Her car was in the driveway twenty minutes later and within half an hour she was roaring off toward the bridge, moderating her speed just in time when she remembered that she still owed Cam for the tire and the service charge.

When she returned several hours later she had in her possession one gown, cocktail length and of sheerest brown cotton with crisp white trim around the slashed neckline and the nonexistent sleeves, one pair of white sandals with three-inch heels and little else, and one very flat purse. There was a grim smile of satisfaction on her face as she swerved her car into its usual parking place and slammed the door resoundingly behind her.

She saw nothing of Cam, Dotty, or Iola all day long, but France wandered over after dinner to complain of boredom. It seemed that Cam had been closed up in his study all day, and when-

ever she had tried to interrupt and cajole him
out to play he had barked at her about falling
back on her own resources.

"I've decided my resources are stagnating
down here," she complained petulantly. "Sometimes I'm sorry I ever came. But then it was so
hot at home and you were here at the beach and
Iola was just as bored after Mr. Harris went to
Germany on business. Anyway, if I hadn't come,
I'd never have met Cam," she finished on a
brighter note, and then, her eyes lighting on the
dress Kate had hung over the back of her door,
she squealed, "Kate, it's fabulous! May I try it
on—pretty please?"

Reluctantly, Kate agreed, and watched while
her ebullient sister slipped the chocolate confec-
tion over her tumble of blond curls. It was
slightly tight and longer on France than on Kate,
but with the blond curls and the large, dark eyes
it was extremely effective.

"Kate, Kitty Kate, may I, please? After all, it's
my special party and I don't even have a new
dress to wear," France pleaded, her full lips
pouting beguilingly.

"Won't you tell me what you're celebrating?"
Kate countered, needing to hear the words,
needing the final cut so that she could begin the
slow healing process.

"Oh, Kate, don't spoil my surprise. Cam and
I . . ."

"All right, all right!" After all, France had
been playing her little roles, dramatizing her
every act all her life, but she would have
thought better of Cameron. "You may have it.
There, try the shoes, too. They won't go with

my navy and green and they're only half a size smaller than you wear." Kate could have screamed in vexation. All her instincts told her to refuse, that just for once in her life she needed to outshine her beautiful younger sister, and it was this unworthy selfishness that made her give in.

At five the next afternoon she saw Iola come scurrying across to Gray Lady. Someone had driven up hurriedly only moments before and Kate supposed that things were getting into full swing over there and that they needed some help. She stood up and put her unread book down, going to meet her mother.

"Need anything?" she called out. Perhaps it was an invitation to dinner. Lord knows, she had refused so many of those lately that they had stopped asking her.

Iola panted dramatically and then, one hand pressed to her bosom, she told Kate that Dotty had had an attack and that the doctor was there now.

After the first few moments of shock, Kate tried to think what to do. She didn't want to be in the way; on the other hand, they could very well be needing someone, especially since both France and Iola tended to fall apart in emergencies. "I'll come back with you. There may be something I can do to help. Do you know how serious it is?" The thought of losing the dear little woman struck her as inconceivable! She knew of no one so young at heart and vital—not even France or Iola.

After seeing the ambulance off with Cam

following in his own car, Kate settled down to phone the guest list and explain the circumstances. France was up in her room and Iola was lying down after Kate had begged a sedative from the doctor for her. She'd probably have to stay over here tonight just to keep an eye on the pair of them, but Cam would be staying at the hospital, no doubt.

The calling all done, Kate made a supper for them, using things that had been prepared for the party. She had had to call the help as well as the guests and now she sat alone in the kitchen with her third cup of coffee and wondered at the outcome of this night.

Cam had called earlier from the hospital to say that Dotty was out of immediate danger but that they were taking her to Elizabeth City and that he'd be along after a while to throw a few things into a bag, and would she wait there, please. France, struggling unsuccessfully to hide her disappointment, had already gone back up to her room. She had hesitated so when Kate asked if she might share it, using the other bed, that Kate had shrugged and said she'd share with Iola instead. Maybe France preferred another roommate—not that Cam would be spending much time with her tonight, probably, for he had told her that he'd be accompanying his grandmother to Elizabeth City.

She'd leave him to break this sad news to her sister. After all, what was a brief disappointment over a cancelled party when weighed against the serious illness of someone they all loved? If Dotty would only pull through and come back home with her usual brash, cheerful impudence, Kate would gladly throw them another party.

It was almost eleven forty-five when Cam returned, and he looked so utterly drained that Kate arose from her chair and went to him instinctively, holding out her hand. He took it, placed it on his forehead for a brief moment, then dropped it to kiss the tips of her fingers before releasing it.

"How is she?" Kate asked, whispering so as not to awaken Iola.

"She's amazing. The last thing she told me before I left was not to let the vol-au-vents go to waste because they wouldn't keep."

A strangled laugh escaped Kate's pale mouth. "Oh, Cam she's priceless! Tell her we put away five for supper and France accounted for three of those." He may as well know about France's healthy appetite, since he'd soon be supporting it. "I gave Iola the sedative and she's doing fine. I looked in on her a few minutes ago. France is still in her room, poor child. She said she was going to read for a while, but I know she's dreadfully disappointed—not that she isn't far more concerned about Dotty, of course," she hastened to add in case he thought his France was unfeeling. Kate had seen little evidence of any concern on her sister's part, but then France was an actress first and foremost and she was probably covering up her deepest feelings so as not to upset Iola any more.

Cameron had loosened his tie and his shirt was unbuttoned almost halfway to his belt. Kate resisted an impulse to run her hands inside the opening and feel that warm, hard body, to offer it all the comfort she could give, but that was not her province and instead she poured him a cup of coffee. "The calls are all made, the food put away, and I fixed a plate for you if you're hungry," she told him.

"Good. I'll just run upstairs first and wash up a bit. I'll have to throw a few things into a bag, and I want to see France. Be down in a minute."

Kate drank a cup of coffee with him, watching with an empty sort of satisfaction while he wolfed his food. At least she could do this much for him. While she had been laying the table in the kitchen she had heard his footsteps overhead, and they had gone directly to France's room, where they had stayed for some five minutes or more. Another five he spent in his own room, and now here he was, looking as if he were trying to juggle a dozen eggs without breaking one. Kate's heart went out to him. "More coffee?"

"God, no! I've consumed gallons tonight. This was great, Katie. One of these days real soon you'll know just what it meant to me to come home and have you waiting here. Right now I've got to rush, and, you may as well know, France is going with me. I'll explain later, when I have more time. I should be back tomorrow night if all goes well."

Something inside her, some tiny seed of hope that had unreasonably begun to raise its head, died a silent death and she only nodded. "Shall Iola and I wait at Gray Lady or would you rather have the whole island to yourself when you get back?"

He gave her a peculiar look, one she didn't even try to interpret. "You'll wait right here! I'll have your promise on that right now!"

She was in no condition to argue, nor was he, so she nodded again, avoiding his eyes when he seemed intent on searching her own for something she didn't dare offer him. It would take a while before she could begin to feel sisterly toward him—a long, long while.

The next day had thirty-six hours in it—all of them empty. It dawned on her that she had another class due in and the idea seemed so irrelevant that she laughed aloud and the sound brought Iola hurrying in from the garden, where she was tying up long-legged chrysanthemums. "What is it?"

"Nothing, Mother." Kate sobered again. "I just now remembered that I have a class due in this afternoon. It had completely slipped my mind, for some reason, what with Dotty and all."

"Oh, Kate, no! Look, sweety, I don't think Cam will want you to go on with your classes. I mean, not under the circumstances. Can't you turn them over to someone else? Or maybe interest them in birdwatching or something they can do on their own? Cam will be back in a little while and he can handle them for you."

"Oh, Iola, be practical for once in your life, will you? Even if I wanted to, even if I could afford to turn them away, you just don't go about canceling classes that have been scheduled for months—not when people have gone to the expense of traveling all this way."

"Well, Cam's not going to like it," Iola warned,

hitching up her aged chiffon negligée to tie a sneaker after removing her workglove. Iola never discarded anything until it was falling around her in rags, and Kate was so used to seeing her gardening and washing windows in chiffon and sleeping in dinner gowns that had gotten too tattered to wear out anywhere that she didn't even think it odd anymore. None of which prevented Iola from indulging in the wildest extravagances when the mood took her, for she rationalized them by pointing out what good wear she got from all her clothes.

Kate finished her lunch and began to wash up the few dishes. "He can just lump it then," she replied tartly. "Look, just because Cam seems to have adopted the pair of you doesn't mean that I don't have a career to think of. If I cancel out on this class, how can I ever expect to sell another series? I'm going over to Gray Lady now and fix a cold supper for them. I'll be there if you need me for anything. In fact, why don't you move over there with me? There's plenty of room—well, Annie's room, at least."

The Capella eyebrows, of which Iola was inordinately proud, rose skyward. "Katie Minerva, how can you? Here Cam will be coming back any minute now and you want him to walk into an empty house? You know, in some ways you're totally unfeeling, Kate. It must have come from your father's side of the family, because we Capellas were never like that."

"Oh, Mother—forget the gene distribution, will you? It's not that I'm unfeeling—you know how much I care for Dotty, and . . . and Cam,

too, but he'll have France with him, and I think
they'll prefer to be alone."

"France? Why on earth should he . . . Has he
called? Did they miss connections?"

"What connections, and no, of course he
didn't call, but—well, I mean, after all . . ."
Kate stammered to a halt. No one had informed her officially of the relationship between Cam and her sister, although just why
they had to make such a production of it,
she couldn't say—unless France was determined to make a big entrance, wearing Kate's
new finery and sporting a ring the size of a
headlight.

Iola assumed an infuriating little smirk, con-
firming Kate's assumption. "Well, it's certainly
not my place to tell you, Katie, dear, but let me
just say this, in case you get upset at the way
we've handled things. Cam knows how you
overreact sometimes when anyone tries to help
out. You see, I told him all about Lawrence and
the way you had stepped in to . . ."

"You what? I do *not* overreact! You know very
well that I've done all I could from the day
Daddy walked out because you always said
I was the strongest one of the family, and
now you stand there and tell me that . . . that
you . . . !"

"There, you see? You're at it again! Darling,
France is twenty-one years old. She's been old
enough to look after herself for ages now, and in
some ways she's a lot more capable than you are,
and I . . ."

Kate's stricken eyes turned blindly away and
her mother stumbled to a halt. Finally, Iola
mumbled something about letting Cam take

care of it, and after a while Kate became aware of being alone again.

The new group came all at once, and when the first two carloads of chattering women pulled up in front of Gray Lady, Kate had to brace herself to greet them with any enthusiasm at all. Within an hour and a half, they had all arrived and were trading experiences and backgrounds, and Kate decided they were going to work just fine. She had enjoyed each group, learned much from teaching them, but somehow, the edge had gone off the whole project. Summer was on the downhill slope and so was she, she decided as she showed them where to stow their gear and set about fixing their meal.

By seven thirty she had them all fed and the rooms buzzed with the echoing sounds of eight voices discussing painting and galleries, inflation and diets, and Kate let herself out the back door and breathed deeply of the scented darkness. Iola had joined them for supper but had returned to Bay Oaks, and Kate saw now that, although there was a light on in her bedroom, she had forgotten to turn the lights on downstairs. Kate had promised to come over and speak to her before bedtime and she could leave the porch light on for Cam when she did.

It had been a long day after a longer night and she might as well get that particular chore out of the way before she turned in. The light southeasterly wind rustled the leaves of the oleanders so that they sounded like rain as Kate crossed the dark area between the two houses. She felt it on her head, still damp from the shower she had taken while the others dealt with the dishes, and

she saw a brief flash of sheet lightning and
wondered if they were in for a squall. Probably another dry shift, Eileen's favorite prog-
nostication whenever a cloud appeared on the
horizon.

Her mind was on alternate plans for tomorrow's class in case it did rain, and when she
looked up in time to see the reddish glow from
the porch, she almost tripped on the bottom
step. "Cam?" she inquired softly, her voice
sounding thin and uncertain.

"I left the light off on account of the bugs." He
appeared at her side and took her arm and she
pulled away as if burned by his touch.

"I can manage, thanks. Where's France?"

"Probably boarding a plane for England about
now," he replied easily.

The words rocked her back on her heels.
"What did you say?"

"I said, pro—"

"Never mind, I heard you, but Cam, why?"
They were on the porch by now and he led her,
unresisting, over to the swing.

"To get the feel of the Continent, I believe was
the way she put it, before her audition."

"Oh, don't be so maddening! Where did she get
the money? I certainly haven't given her enough
for the fare, much less . . ."

"I gave it to her," he answered with infuriating calmness.

Kate's automatic response was explosive, but
she managed to choke it off after the first sputter
of indignation. After all, if Cam wanted to spend
his money that way, it was no concern of hers.
"You might at least have told me," she muttered.

"We didn't tell you because we all knew exactly how you'd react."

"You mean you've all discussed me—talked about . . ." She bit her lip to still the trembling. "You have some kind of a flattering impression of me, don't you?" she accused bitterly. Her face was beginning to crumple and a thickness had invaded her throat as she drove her fingernails into the palms of her hands fiercely.

"Kate, if things had gone according to my plans, we wouldn't be sitting out here getting ready to fight again, I can assure you, but . . ."

"Oh, of that I'm certain! It's just too bad that you're not halfway to England with my sister! What will you do—fly over as soon as . . . Oh, Cam! Dotty! I didn't even ask!"

"She's fine," he told her with a laugh that made the goose bumps rise on her arms. He dropped an arm across her shoulder and pulled her stiff body against his. "Dotty's just fine. She'll be coming home again next weekend and I've already made arrangements with Eileen to live in and look after her for a few weeks."

"If you need an extra hand, I can pop in between classes," she offered, tacitly apologizing for her outburst.

"You'll have your hands full, I hope—getting ready for something else," he told her, his deep voice wrought with something she didn't understand.

When she didn't reply, he turned to look at her, and in the ambient light she felt, rather than saw, his look of inquiry. "Well, aren't you going to ask me what I mean?" he teased.

"If you want me to know, I assume you'll tell me," she retorted primly, and he laughed again, a softer sound that affected her senses even more, and she decided she'd better go inside before she did anything foolish. "Iola . . . I told her . . ." she began, and he pressed a finger across her lips.

"Kate . . . Kate Minerva Capella Brown, will you marry me as soon as it is legally possible and put an end to this inept, mismanaged, farcical courtship?"

"This . . . will I . . . ?"

He sighed heavily. "There, you see? I try the direct approach and instead of a simple yes I get a 'this' and a 'will I'. Your family warned me you weren't exactly an easy proposition. I'm not certain it wasn't a mistake to take their advice."

"Cameron Greyville, just what in the devil are you talking about? If this is your idea of a joke, then I . . . then you . . ." Her voice wobbled off into limbo and to her horror she heard a noisy sob escape her. She turned her face away from him and tried to gain her feet, but she was prevented from escaping by the increased pressure of his arm.

"Katie? Darling, what is it? Have I hurt your feelings? I didn't mean to be clumsy about it, but, sweetheart, I've never done this sort of thing before. These past few days have been such a strain, it's a wonder I didn't just say to hell with it and drag you off to the nearest preacher."

She was unable to prevent a watery smile at the mental picture, but her voice wasn't up to the task of replying, and when he turned her deftly so that she lay half across his lap, she burrowed her face in the warm, clean-smelling flesh at the throat of his open shirt.

"Katie? What's it going to be, love—wedded bliss or a life of glorious sin? I'll go either way—whatever it takes to make you finally and completely mine." He caught her chin and lifted her face, glowing warmly down at her in the soft, starlighted darkness. His lips touched the corner of her mouth, then slid lightly over her lips to the other corner, and when she would have caught his head and put a definite end to his tantalizing butterfly kiss, he shook his head. "No more until you give me an answer, Katie Minerva. Iola says you do, France says you don't, and Dotty says I'm a fool if I let you get away. Well? Do you? Will you?"

"Oh, Cam, I love you so terribly much I'll do anything you want me to. I thought you knew— although I hoped to heaven you didn't."

"But why, precious? Why couldn't you have given me a hint instead of acting like a blooming little cactus whenever I tried to get near you?"

She leaned away from him and snorted in a ladylike way. "Ha! As I remember it, everytime you got near me you tried to . . . you almost . . . well, you know!"

He threw back his head and roared, his laughter mingling with the scent of sun-warmed groundsel, wax myrtle, and salt water. "I tried to what? I almost what? If you mean I did my best to make love to you, then let me remind you that you were only one step behind me every time."

Before she could protest, he gathered her up in his arms and proceeded to demonstrate, and by the time he lifted his mouth from hers, she could only nod weakly. "You win," she said shakily.

"No, darling, we both win—although I'll concede that I'm the biggest winner. After all, once

I made up my mind to have you, it was only a matter of time."

"How could I have been fool enough to fall in love with such an insufferably smug creature?" she crowed, covering the hand that had crept up to cover her breast—the breast that covered a heart that was full to overflowing. "When *did* you make up your mind?" she asked almost timidly then.

"Somewhere between the first and the second kiss," he growled against her throat. Then, lifting his head, he added, "But once I tried to do something about it and almost ran afoul of that suit of defensive armor you wear, I had to back off and try a bit of strategy. For one thing, I knew I had to get your wacky, loveable, but unfortunately dependent family off your neck so you wouldn't reject me and do the martyr bit. I couldn't have handled a rejection from you, love. It seemed to me that it would be easier to solve all your problems and then sweep you off your feet, only things got all fouled up along the way."

"Poor Saint George," she cooed. "And here I was trying my darnedest to keep a stiff upper lip and learn to call you brother-in-law. Did you know that?"

He didn't, and by the time she had elaborated, he felt another demonstration was in order. "Your mother explained to me, darling, about your father and his lady friends," he told her much later.

"That was why I didn't dare let myself trust you. Mother went right on loving my father even when he practically paraded his . . . his girls in front of her, but I could never share you. Never!

It hurt me too much every time I saw the way you were with Bebe and Stella and even France," she confessed. "Mother said some men were made that way, though. They could never be satisfied with a single flower when the whole garden was in bloom."

"Darling, the other women in my life meant about as much to me as the pictures in a seed catalog. France is a pretty scamp—spoiled, mischievous, and a thorough brat—although with a woman like Iola for a mother, there's hope for her. You have no more cause for worry about any other woman than I have about Brookwood or Palani or any other poor unfortunate male in your lurid past. There's only one Kate Minerva Brown—fiercely independent, warm, and loving, with an overdeveloped sense of responsibility and an irreverent sense of humor—and she's mine, promised to me way back in the beginning of time."

"You're right about one thing, at least," Katie told him breathlessly. "Whatever she is, she's yours." Her arms crept up around his neck, and just before his face blocked out the starlight, she caught a gleam of amber eyes that promised several lifetimes of enchantment.

Silhouette Romance

IT'S YOUR OWN SPECIAL TIME

Contemporary romances for today's women.
Each month, six very special love stories will be yours
from SILHOUETTE.
Look for them wherever books are sold
or order now from the coupon below.

$1.50 each

Silhouette Romance

- - - - - - - - - - - - - - - - - - - -

SILHOUETTE BOOKS. Department SB/1

1230 Avenue of the Americas
New York, NY 10020

Please send me the books I have checked above. I am enclosing
$_____ (please add 50¢ to cover postage and handling. NYS and
NYC residents please add appropriate sales tax). Send check or
money order—no cash or C.O.D.'s please. Allow six weeks for delivery.

NAME_____

ADDRESS_____

CITY_____STATE/ZIP_____

15-Day Free Trial Offer
6 Silhouette Romances

6 Silhouette Romances, free for 15 days! We'll send you 6 new Silhouette Romances to keep for 15 days, absolutely free! If you decide not to keep them, send them back to us. You pay nothing.

Free Home Delivery. But if you enjoy them as much as we think you will, keep them by paying us the retail price of just $1.50 each. We'll pay all shipping and handling charges. You'll then automatically become a member of the Silhouette Book Club, and will receive 6 more new Silhouette Romances every month and a bill for $9.00. That's the same price you'd pay in the store, but you get the convenience of home delivery.

Read every book we publish. The Silhouette Book Club is the way to make sure you'll be able to receive every new romance we publish.

This offer expires January 31, 1982

Silhouette Book Club, Dept. SBF17B
120 Brighton Road, Clifton, NJ 07012

Please send me 6 Silhouette Romances to keep for 15 days, absolutely free. I understand I am not obligated to join the Silhouette Book Club unless I decide to keep them.

NAME_____

ADDRESS_____

CITY_____ STATE_____ ZIP_____

READERS' COMMENTS ON SILHOUETTE ROMANCES:

"Your books are written with so much feeling and quality that they make you feel as if you are part of the story."

—D.C.*, Piedmont, SC

"I'm very particular about the types of romances I read; yours more than fill my thirst for reading."

—C.D., Oxford, MI

"I hope Silhouette novels stay around for many years to come. . . . Keep up the good work."

—P.C., Frederick, MD

"What a relief to be able to escape in a well-written romantic story."

—E.N., Santa Maria, CA

"Silhouette Romances . . . Fantastic!"

—M.D., Bell, CA

"I'm pleased to be adding your books to my collection—my library is growing in size every day."

—B.L., La Crescenta, CA

* Names available on request.